Aussie
STEM Stars

VEENA SAHAJWALLA

'Green' engineer and recycling champion

Story told by JULIANNE NEGRI

Aussie STEM Stars series
Published by Wild Dingo Press
Melbourne, Australia
books@wilddingopress.com.au
wilddingopress.com.au

This work was first published by Wild Dingo Press 2022

Cover Design: Gisela Beer
Illustrations: Mirjana Segan
Series Editor: Catherine Lewis
Printed in Australia.

Negri, Julianne 1971–, author.
Veena Sahajwalla: 'Green' engineer and recycling champion / Julianne Negri

A catalogue record for this book is available from the National Library of Australia

ISBN: 9781925893250 (paperback)
ISBN: 9781925893243 (epdf)
ISBN: 9781925893229 (epub)

I see problems as opportunities. I'm excited about all the innovative solutions I could be developing to solve our environmental challenges – anything is possible!

— *Veena Sahajwalla*

Contents

1

Mumbai streets

Do you remember being three years old?

Veena Sahajwalla does.

She remembers this: she was small but felt big. Her hair, dark, thick and wavy, bounced around her face and she pushed the fringe out of her eyes. She was outside with her parents on the noisy streets of **Mumbai**, and she was allowed to stand on the floorboard of her father's Vespa scooter while he stood by and held the bike firmly. The scooter was bright blue and shiny. Standing on the step-through floorboard, Veena reached her hands up to hold the handlebars but could barely see over the top. She stood on her tiptoes to peer over.

'Vroom vroom! I want to go for a ride! Vroom!'

'Ah, you want to take it for a spin?' said her father. Veena's eyes lit up and, jumping up and down, she shouted, 'Yes, yes, yes! Please, Daddy! Let's go!'

With a rumbling chuckle, her father sat down on the seat behind her, making the Vespa rock a little.

'Hold on!' he said, as he turned the key and started the scooter's engine. Her father held the handlebars, his big hands next to her small ones. He revved the engine before kicking up the stand and pushing off, lifting his feet and placing them on the floorboard, his knees either side of Veena's small frame holding her in like a safety harness. They were away, rumbling through the streets of Mumbai!

Veena could feel the vibration of the engine through her feet and the wind flying in her thick black hair. She tilted her face to the sun and smiled widely until her cheeks hurt. It was wonderful! She was free! They didn't go fast but, to Veena at three years old, they were zooming though the streets!

Her body swayed with the turning scooter as it weaved in and out of traffic that seemed to be going in all directions at once. Veena looked around with fascination; she was in it, amongst it, part of it – the hustle the bustle, the hubbub, that is Mumbai, her home.

From the scooter she could see that what seemed a blur of traffic, comprised of buses, trucks, cars, motorbikes, all sorts of vehicles tooting horns and revving engines. People darted in and out, shouting and calling to each other while bicycles swirled through, bells dinging furiously. It all combined in a percussive, trancelike noise that enveloped her. They passed a cart being pulled by an ox, his horns long and sharp. Veena squealed with delight. It was wonderful!

She breathed in the air, wafting with spices and fried oil from the food stalls and heady diesel fumes from the vehicles. She looked up towards the overcast sky and saw balconies draped with washing and children calling down to their friends below. Veena waved and grinned. The footpath teemed with people. Some in western dress, jeans and dresses, some in brightly patterned saris, a mash-up of culture and colour.

A **sari** is a garment traditionally worn by women in India, Sri Lanka, Pakistan, Bangladesh and Nepal. It is a piece of cotton or silk, 4-8 metres long, worn round the body with one end over the head or shoulder.

A woman in a hot pink **sari**, a wide basket balanced on her head, walked gracefully across the road just in front of them, the shiny silk shimmering as she moved. She saw men carrying towers of suitcases on their heads. The streets were bursting with buying, selling, repairing, making, cooking, animals and so many wheels – wheels on carts, bicycles, barrows, cars, buses and scooters. And was that a cow resting on the footpath? Veena laughed. 'Moo!' she shouted as they passed.

It wasn't chaos to Veena's three-year-old mind. This was Mumbai. Her home. The bustling city that created neural pathways in her mind that would forever be able to see patterns in chaos, be impatient for things to happen fast, and see value in what others would throw away. This bright three-year-old, taking in all around her, would grow up to become a recycling champion, inventor of green steel, the innovative scientist who would envisage economic solutions for recycling in small communities and sustainability in large manufacturing.

But for now, she was Veena – a girl who enjoyed going fast, loved her family, was always thinking, and whose megawatt smile lit up every room she entered.

Mumbai was called Bombay until 1995. It is the biggest city in India with 21 million people. It is so densely populated that there is only 1.28 metres of open space per person. It is the home of India's famous film industry, Bollywood and, like New York, it is known as the city that never sleeps. The city also produces more than 10,000 tonnes of rubbish a day.

2

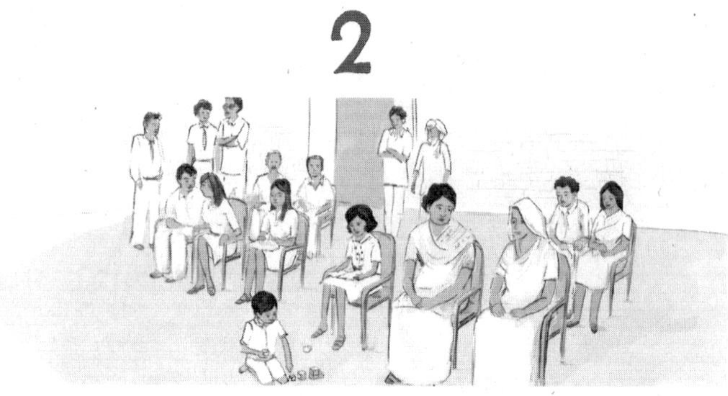

Mother's footsteps

Veena's mother was always the first in the house to be awake. She moved fast and efficiently to get housework done and breakfast cooked before going to work at a local clinic where she worked as a doctor, looking after the families in the community. Although small in stature, she was a powerhouse of knowledge, composure, and care. Veena's father worked as an engineer, helping to construct the burgeoning city that Veena so loved. He was also up early, getting ready to go into the city to work.

Rolling out of bed, Veena grabbed her doll. She loved the doll's dark, short curly hair, smooth plastic skin, the way her arms and legs moved and especially the long-lashed blinking eyes. She thought of her doll as her friend. It was a school day and she needed to get ready too.

Stumbling into the kitchen, sleepy-eyed, her doll under her arm, she could smell the warm ***parathas*** and her stomach rumbled. Her mother placed a glass of milk on the table which she gulped down while watching her parents. She admired them both so much and knew that their work was very important.

'Go and wake your brother up, Veena,' said her mother. Veena was seven years old and often helped out with her younger brother, Ashu. Before she left the table, her father bent down and gave her a kiss.

'Time for me to get to work!' he said, grabbing his briefcase and heading out the door. 'Have a good day at school, Veena!'

Veena used her doll's arm to wave goodbye before finishing her milk.

'Let's wake up Ashu,' she said to her doll.

At her brother's bedroom door she called, 'Wake up, sleepy head!'

There was no time for sleeping in. They had to get ready for school. Veena liked school. She enjoyed learning and the friendships of the other children. She especially loved maths. She felt a thrilling excitement when working with numbers. It was magic.

Before and after school, Veena and Ashu spent time at the surgery where their mother worked. Veena didn't mind at all and neither did Ashu, especially because their mother was a **paediatrician,** and the waiting room was full of toys and children's books. Devika, the receptionist, always made a fuss of them too.

A **paediatrician** is a specialist doctor of children's health care.

'Here's our big Dr Sahajwalla and our little Dr Sahajwalla too,' said Devika as soon they arrived. Veena smiled and grew a little taller, almost bursting with pride at being considered a smaller version of her amazing mother.

'Now, you stay out of the way and don't be any trouble,' said her mother. 'And watch Ashu too.'

'Of course!' said Veena flashing her smile. But watching over her younger brother wasn't her top priority. In fact, she hoped he would occupy himself with the toys.

Veena sat on the chair in the waiting room, kicking her legs, impatient for the surgery to open.

Eventually, the phone started ringing and families came through the door. She was intrigued with the people in the waiting room, wondering about their lives and stories. To Veena, the surgery was a fascinating place. She liked watching as her mother helped the children, all with her trademark efficiency and, even though she loved school, it was always hard to drag herself away in the morning. School seemed so boring compared to the ongoing dramas of her mother's surgery. Devika kept her eye on the time and told them when they had to leave, checking they had their schoolbags as she saw them out the door.

'See you this afternoon,' Veena said, looking over her shoulder to see the children entering the surgery. Ashu pulled on her arm. 'Come on, Veena, we don't want to be late.'

By the time Veena and Ashu walked back into their mother's work after school, the waiting room was full of people. Before opening the door, Veena could hear babies crying, toddlers whimpering and the phone ringing. While weaving through the people to find a place to sit, Veena wanted to reassure them all, *'It's going to be okay, my mummy is going to make you better'*. Many of the families smiled at Veena, knowing that she was Dr Sahajwalla's daughter.

Ashu went straight for the blocks and began making a city with tall buildings and driving a small car around them. Veena sat down and pulled out her book to read and watched as a young girl about her age, went in to see her mother. The girl looked sad and sick, and her parents' faces showed they were worried. Veena looked back to her book but couldn't really concentrate. Was the girl going to be alright?

A little while later, she heard the door open and looked up.

'Thank you so much, Doctor,' the father was saying. Both parents were thanking her mother profusely, looking relieved and the girl was smiling now. Veena knew it was her mother who had made that difference. She felt so proud and nudged Ashu.

'Did you see that? Mummy made that girl better!'

Ashu smiled back at her. They were both proud of their mother.

Dr Sahajwalla briefly waved to them before seeing the next patient. She was always very busy. A woman next to Veena said, 'Are you going to be a doctor like your wonderful mother when you grow up?' Veena smiled and shrugged her shoulders. Sometimes she thought, yes, I want to be amazing like my mother. And other times she wondered if she could ever be that clever? Even though she smiled and nodded when people asked her, deep down she wasn't so sure.

She already knew she was expected to follow in her mother's footsteps. Those footsteps, though! They were fast! And never seemed to stop! Her mother got up early, worked around the house before anyone else was awake, made the food and kept everything tidy. She went to the surgery early before it opened and saw patients all day and made diagnoses and important decisions to help sick children. She healed them, stitched them up, gave medicine and needles. She dealt with problems and emergencies each and every day. Whatever the situation was, Veena's mother seemed to know the right thing to do, immediately, and without a fuss. And then after all that, she came home and looked after Veena, Ashu and their Daddy. Her mother was never confused or unsure.

In bed that night, Veena couldn't sleep, so she sat up to play with her doll. She brushed the doll's thick dark hair and wrapped a rag of fabric around her for a blanket.

'Do you think I'll be a doctor?' she asked her doll. She rocked her so the heavy-lashed eyes blinked twice.

'Yes, I don't know either,' said Veena and she blinked twice back. Veena tucked the blanket around her doll and lay her down on the pillow next to her. The doll's eyes closed as she lay back.

'Asleep already?' said Veena. And she closed her eyes too, and quickly fell to sleep too.

Like so many people in this huge densely packed city, the Sahajwalla family lived in an apartment. Theirs was on the upper floor of a big building where they had a balcony overlooking the other apartments. Veena liked living in a busy city. It was the hub of activity in India, a city heaving with industry, factories, people and traffic. A city full of possibilities. But she also liked to escape into the quiet of her bedroom and read and daydream.

'Veena! Ashu! Come and play!' called a voice.

Together they went to the balcony. Ashu stood on his tippy toes to try and see.

'Are you coming down, Veena? We need someone to bowl!' the voice called.

Their downstairs neighbour, Rishi, was waving his cricket bat with his left hand and tossing a ball up and catching it with his right. The good thing about living in the apartments was that there was always someone to play with. The children often played together in a group or teams – games of skippy, hopscotch, elastics, or huge games of chasey, and always…cricket.

'Let's go!' cried Ashu.

'We're coming!' she shouted down to Rishi. Ashu jumped for joy. 'You can be wicketkeeper,' she said to him.

Being a dutiful older sister, Veena took Ashu downstairs to join the others, knowing how much he would enjoy himself. Veena enjoyed playing with the other children too, but sometimes, just sometimes, she wanted to stay in her room, read a book or just think and dream.

When Ashu grew tired of chasing the cricket ball they went back to their apartment, hot and hungry. The house smelt of fresh lemons from the folded washing and everything was tidy. Bipasha was there. She sometimes came to help with the housework.

'Hello, Bipasha!' they both called. Ashu got himself a big glass of water. 'The house smells so good when you're here!' said Veena taking a deep breath.

Ashu threw himself onto the rug and played with his little cars, taking them out of the shoebox and broom-brooming them to and fro across the floor at high speed, chasing them and retrieving them from under the furniture.

Bipasha smiled and said, 'I've finished all the work. I think it is time for a cup of tea.'

'Oh, yes, please!' sighed Veena. 'All that cricket has made me quite tired.'

She loved a sweet cup of tea and biscuits in the afternoons with Bipasha. Bipasha poured three cups of **chai tea**, sweetened with condensed milk.

'There's nothing better than a cup of tea after a hard day's work,' sighed Veena.

'You're a funny one, little Veena. Wise beyond your years.'

All three sat together on the floor and sipped the warm spicy tea. Veena closed her eyes and sighed as the milky liquid coated her mouth, slowly releasing the caramel sweetness.

'I love sweet things,' Veena said.

'I know,' laughed Bipasha, passing her another biscuit and patting her knee. 'Me too.'

3

The case of the coconut

Veena lay on her bed, totally lost in a **Sherlock Holmes** mystery, when she felt a tug on her foot.

'Yes, Ashu?' she said, without looking up.

'Veena!' he pestered, 'I'm hungry. Can you open the coconut?'

'Have a banana,' she said, glued to the mystery book.

But the tugging continued.

'Please, Veena!' he pleaded. 'I want coconut.' He pushed the brown hairy coconut up to her face.

'Can't Bipasha get you something to eat?'

'She's already gone home. Please, Veena,' said Ashu.

Veena looked longingly at the words dancing on the page, enticing her to solve the mystery, and then at the coconut Ashu held out to her. She slid a bookmark onto the page and closed the book, shutting Sherlock Holmes, Dr Watson and the adventure inside. She sat up and turned her attention to the task at hand.

Taking the coconut from her brother, Veena bounced it in her hands while she considered the problem. A coconut. Hard shell. Sweet water and white flesh inside. Her stomach grumbled. 'Yum!' she said as she stood up.

Did you know: coconuts are not nuts? They belong to the stone-fruit family. A coconut palm can grow up to 30 metres so the coconut has evolved to survive falling all that distance. It has an extra fibrous husk called the pericarp that grows up to 10 cm thick. Underneath the pericarp is the fibrous brown shell that is extremely hard.

'Let's see. How to solve the mystery of the coconut.' Rolling it in her hands, she carefully inspected it from every angle.

'It's not a mystery,' said Ashu. 'You just have to open it and let me eat it.'

'That's right,' said Veena. 'I just have to open it. But how?'

She knocked on the coconut with her knuckles.

'Sounds like knocking on wood,' Ashu said.

'Elementary, my dear Ashu! That means the coconut is very hard.' She held it out for him and he knocked on it twice.

'Knock, knock,' said Ashu.

'Who's there?' Veena replied.

'Wooden shoe.'

'Wooden shoe who?' asked Veena.

'Wooden shoe like to hear another joke?'

They both laughed.

'That's a good one,' said Veena. 'And yes, I would like to hear another joke.'

'Okay, how about this one. Knock, knock,' Ashu said, knocking on the coconut.

'Who's there?' asked Veena.

'Atch,' said Ashu.

'Atch who?' asked Veena.

'Bless you!' shouted Ashu. 'Do you need a handkerchief?'

Once she recovered from the giggles, Veena got serious.

'Right,' she said. 'Enough joking. Just how are we going to open this coconut, hmm?'

'Mummy uses the big cleaver,' pointed out Ashu.

Veena looked over at the huge heavy blade in the kitchen but shook her head.

'No, I don't think so,' she said. 'That's too dangerous for us. I would chop off my finger and have to get Mummy to sew it back on again! There has to be another way. We just have to think.' Veena tapped her brother on the head. 'Are you thinking?' she asked.

'Yes,' he answered with a serious thinking frown on his face.

Veena tilted her head to the left. She tilted her head on the right.

'We need to smash it open,' she said suddenly. 'Stand back!' And with that she threw the coconut down to the floor.

BANG!

It made a loud crash before rolling away. Ashu crawled under a chair to grab it.

'Is it cracked?' Veena called to him, full of optimism.

'No. It's still in one piece.'

'Worth a try,' she shrugged as Ashu handed the coconut back to her. Veena carefully inspected the whole surface, turning it in her hand.

'Not even a crack!' she said. 'It needs more force. I know. How about I drop it from somewhere higher?'

'Good idea,' Ashu said.

Veena pulled out a chair and climbed up.

'Stand back,' she said again, Ashu ran and crouched behind the sofa, peeking out to watch. Veena held the coconut high above her head and said, 'Ready, set, go!'

BANG!

The coconut hit the floor and rolled away once more with Ashu chasing it.

'Is it cracked this time?' called Veena.

Ashu shook his head as he gave it back to her, saying, 'Maybe I'll just have a banana'.

But Veena wouldn't give up now.

'No way! We're going to find a way to break this thing!' she said with steely determination. 'I'll try throwing it from even higher. I have to think.'

A frown creased her forehead. Then it disappeared and a grin spread across her face.

'Aha!' she cried. 'No banana for you! You will have coconut, Ashu! I have a plan,' she declared, glaring at the coconut. Veena and the coconut were locked in a battle now, and she was determined to win. She was also finding the process of experimenting and failing totally absorbing. Trying one thing, noting that it doesn't work, thinking of the how and why, and coming up with another plan. It was absolutely thrilling.

'Go downstairs and into the garden,' she said to her little brother. 'I'm going to stand on the balcony and throw it down from here! Let's see if being even higher works!'

'Good plan!' shouted Ashu excitedly as he ran out the door.

While Veena waited for him to get to the garden, she closely inspected the coconut. Was there a weak spot? Her mother always cut coconuts along the side, so she decided to aim for it to land that way too, on the side.

'I'm ready, Veena!'

'Move out of the way,' she called. 'Here it comes. One...two...three!'

And there it went. Over the rail, falling fast down the side of the building. Veena's heart was in her throat while she watched. Would it work?

CRASH!

It landed in the bushes.

'Well?' she called down impatiently. 'Did I do it? Is it at least cracked?'

Ashu climbed into the bushes to retrieve the fruit and looked it over closely before looking up and shaking his head sadly, holding the coconut aloft to show her it was still in one piece. Veena slumped against the balcony. Ashu ran back upstairs and handed it to her.

Not to be defeated, she paced around the apartment thinking about it some more. Ashu imitated her and paced and thought too. *Throwing it from somewhere higher hasn't worked*, she thought, looking over the coconut surface. *The coconut is so hard that perhaps it needs to hit something hard!*

It was a lightbulb moment.

'Something hard needs to collide with something hard in order to break!' she shouted. 'A hammer is hard and breaks things. A pick can break rocks. We have to hit this against something hard. What is the hardest thing in the house?'

'The coconut?' said Ashu.

'Very funny!' said Veena.

Then she had another light bulb moment.

'The sink!' she said.

The kitchen sink was made from hard ceramic. When she had accidentally dropped a cup in there another time it had smashed to smithereens.

Ashu and Veena stood by the sink.

'What do you think, little brother? Will this work?'

'I hope so,' he answered. 'I'm very hungry now.'

'This is just as hard as the coconut, see?' she said knocking on the sink

'Knock, knock,' said Ashu

'Who's there?' asked Veena

'Cows go.'

'Cows go who?'

'No, silly, cows go MOO!' Ashu shouted.

'Another good one. But now, let's do this!'

Veena decided that height plus a hard surface together might just be the answer. She dragged over the chair and climbed up on the kitchen bench. Taking a deep breath, she held the coconut high above her head once more.

'One... two... three!'

She threw the coconut down as hard as she could on the edge of the sink.

SMASH!

Ashu let out a shriek! Veena's hands flew to her mouth! 'Oh, no!'

'What have you done!' cried Ashu, eyes wide as saucers.

Veena couldn't believe her eyes. She knelt down on the bench because her legs felt a bit wobbly. The edge of the sink had broken off completely and there was a huge crack running right through the entire centre of the sink. And there, on the floor, rolled the coconut. Still in one piece.

'You broke it, Veena! You broke the kitchen sink! Just wait until Mummy gets home!' Ashu squeaked.

'Quick, get the coconut, Ashu.'

Together they look it over. Not even a crack! Not even a scratch!

Veena climbed down and sat on the floor with her back to the kitchen cupboard. Their mother should be home any minute.

'Are you still hungry?' asked Veena

'Yes,' answered Ashu.

'Why not have a banana,' suggested Veena.

Ashu got a banana, peeled it, and gobbled it up. Veena was still thinking about the problem of the coconut. Now that she was over the shock, she found it interesting that the ceramic broke with the force of the coconut.

'Are you worried about getting in trouble?' Ashu asked her.

'A little,' answered Veena. 'But it's been an interesting experiment.'

'It would have been better if it worked,' said Ashu.

'Perhaps.'

Just then, they heard their mother come home. They stood up next to each other in front of the sink. Should they tell her straightaway? Veena's mother put her bag on the table and then saw the two of them standing there, the coconut in their hands. She knew from their downcast gaze that something was wrong.

'What has happened here?' she asked. 'Are you both alright? Is anyone hurt?'

Veena reassured her mother, 'We're fine, Mummy, but...'

'I was hungry for coconut...' began Ashu.

'And I tried to find a way to open it,' explained Veena.

'She tried and tried and didn't give up,' said Ashu proudly. 'Veena can be very determined.'

'Yes, I know. And then what happened?' asked their mother.

They both turned and silently pointed to the sink. Veena looked down at the broken sink and the large crack in the surface. She almost hoped it wouldn't be as bad as she thought. But it was.

'I threw it and broke the sink,' Veena said. 'I'm sorry, Mummy.'

Veena's mother pushed through them to see.

'It is completely smashed!' she gasped. 'It will have to be replaced!'

Veena held up the coconut to her mother and knocked on it. 'It's a very hard coconut. See?'

Veena's mother sighed and took the coconut.

'Look,' she said gathering the two children close to her.

'You've made a light crack in the surface. Right here.'

Veena's eyes lit up. She was delighted! 'Really? I have?'

'Who wants some coconut?' their mother asked.

'I do!' shouted Ashu.

Veena's mother took it to the bench and got out the cleaver. While Ashu and Veena watched, she expertly tapped the coconut around the middle with the blunt side…tap, tap, tap, tap and then… finally… it split open.

She poured out the coconut water into two glasses.

'Here you go,' she said, passing them to the children.

They drank it up with gusto.

'Want to hear a knock-knock joke?' asked Ashu.

'Of course!' said their mother.

Veena looked at the inside of the coconut. The shell wasn't very thick but so strong. She brought a piece up to her mouth and bit the flesh, stripping it from the shell with her sharp bottom teeth. Delicious.

When her father came home and saw the cracked sink, he was angry at first.

'How on earth did this happen? We'll have to buy a whole new sink!'

When Veena and Ashu related the whole story to him – of how they tried to break the coconut but only succeeded in breaking the sink – his eyes sparkled as he listened, a smile itching at the corners of his mouth.

'And you thought of all those ways to try to break it?' he said to Veena.

She nodded.

'That shows you have a good creative brain,' he said. 'And best of all, it shows real tenacity!'

'What does tenacity mean?' she asked.

'Tenacity means that you don't give up,' he answered smiling.

'Or another word for it could be stubbornness!' called out her mother, putting a plastic basin into the sink as a replacement until it could get fixed.

Veena folded her arms and nodded.

'Tenacity,' she said. 'I like it.'

That night when Veena was in bed she thought about the coconut. It felt terrible to break something in the house but she couldn't help but feel a fizzle of excitement about how much fun it was to experiment. To try things, fail, come up with ideas and think about the problem some more; to go deeper into a problem in order to solve it. That was all rather thrilling.

4

When I grow up

Veena and Sonali sat together on a bench in the school playground.

'Open your lunchbox very slowly,' Veena said. 'I want to savour each layer.'

Veena's family was different from her best friend's family. This was most obvious at school lunchtimes. Veena bought her lunch at the canteen because her mother was too busy for homemade lunches, but Sonali had homemade lunches every day, all packed in a round shiny silver steel lunchbox, called a tiffin, stacked up in layers. Veena's favourite part of the school day was watching as Sonali lifted the lid of each compartment and seeing what she had. And best of all, Sonali always shared.

Sonali opened each layer, watching as her friend's eyes widened and sparkled. Veena made 'ooh' and 'ah' noises as each layer was revealed – rice, dried vegetables, **dahl** and **dosa**, and sometimes **chapati**, **idli** and **bhaaji**.

Dahl: a spicy stew made from lentils, peas or legumes.

Dosa: a thin savoury pancake made from ground rice, ground lentils and salt.

Chapati: a flat bread made from wheat and water.

Idli: a round steamed rice cake.

Bhaaji: a fried vegetable fritter.

'Oh, wow! So amazing! Your lunches are so delicious!' Veena exclaimed, groaning and rolling on the bench, her stomach rumbling loudly. Sonali laughed and offered her some **dosa**. Veena tore a piece off and let it melt in her mouth.

'Your mummy is such a good cook!'

'Yes, I am very lucky!' Sonali replied. 'But so are you. Your mummy is clever. Everyone knows her.

She's the best doctor around.'

'Yes, but your mummy makes the best lunches ever!'

They shared each layer. And at the end, Sonali said, 'Here, have a **kaju kibarfi**!'

Kaju kibarfi are sweets made with cashews, ghee, cardamom and sugar and cut into diamond shapes. They are a whitish colour and delicious.

'Oh, yes, please. I love sweets!'

'I know,' smiled Sonali. 'That's why I always ask for two pieces. Do you want to come to my house today after school?' she continued.

'Is your mummy cooking today?'

'She is,' Sonali assured her.

'I'll come! Mmm, mmm!' said Veena, nodding, her mouth melting with sugary nuts and fatty ghee. Sonali grinned back.

In class that day they were divided into groups and told to work out a play about their future. Veena rolled her eyes.

'Why does everyone want to know what we will be when we grow up?' she asked.

She didn't really know what she wanted to do with her life. Who does at ten years old? But the rest of the group, Sonali, Priya and Sangita, were taking the assignment seriously. They were allowed to work outside for this exercise, so they spread out over the playground and found a bench in the shade to sit on.

'Let's just get this organised,' said Sangita. 'I want to get a good mark from Miss Mishra.'

Sonali took a pen from her pencil case and opened her exercise book. 'I'll write the plan down so we don't forget,' she said.

Veena sighed and fidgeted. She stood up and did some star jumps and said, 'I think we should make this play exciting. Make it into something different! Make it dramatic!'

'Veena, just do what you're told,' Priya said, exasperatedly.

But Veena looked around, distracted. She wanted to know what the other groups were doing.

'I'm going to go and spy on the others. Let's see what they're up to!' She ran off before the girls could try to stop her.

While Veena was gone the rest of the group continued.

'What will you be, Sonali?' asked Sangita.

'I don't know for sure. Maybe a nurse. Or a kindergarten teacher. I like little children. They're funny. I've helped out with so many of my little brothers and sisters, I think I already know what to do.'

Sangita didn't like that idea.

'Little kids are always whining and have snotty noses,' she said.

'*I* don't think so!' said Sonali.

'Well, you have to pick just one profession with snotty children. What will it be?'

'Um, midwife!' Sonali declared and wrote it down. She smiled to herself. Yes, she liked the idea of delivering babies very much.

'Well, what about you? What are you going to be?' Sonali asked Sangita.

'Me? I love big, complicated numbers!' Sangita said. 'I think I'll be an accountant. And I can happily do sums all day.'

'Perfect!' said Sonali writing that down. 'You can have a pretend calculator in the play and be working out sums. We'll get you lots of books to carry.'

'What about you, Priya?' asked Sonali, pen ready.

'I'm going to be Prime Minister,' she answered seriously. 'Just like **Indira Gandhi**.'

Indira Gandhi was the daughter of India's first prime minister, Jawaharlal Nehru. She was the first and only female prime minister in India: from 1966 to 1977, and again from 1980 to 1984, when she was assassinated. She was prime minister for some of Veena's childhood.

The others raised their eyebrows and whistled through their teeth. 'That's ambitious!' Sangita said.

'I'll write down politician,' said Sonali. 'And in the play, you can be doing a speech at a rally.'

'So, it will be just before I become Prime Minister?' said Priya.

'Exactly,' said Sonali, adding it to her list.

'We'll make a voting poster as a prop!' Sangita said excitedly. 'Vote one, Priya!'

Priya beamed at the idea. 'Oh yes,' she said. 'I like that!'

Veena came running back, breathless.

'What did you find out?' asked Sonali.

'All the boys want to be cricketers or engineers,' she told them.

'And you?' asked Sangita. 'You'll be a doctor like your mother, right?'

'Hmmm,' said Veena. 'I'm not sure. What have the rest of you decided?'

Sonali read from the list.

'I'm going to be a midwife, Sangita is going to be an accountant and Priya is going to be a politician.'

'You mean, Prime Minister,' interrupted Priya. 'Change it to Prime Minister.'

'I love that, Priya! My friend, the Prime Minster!' declared Veena.

'So, there's just you left, Veena,' said Sangita.

'Well, I just did some excellent spying,' said Veena. 'So maybe I'll be a spy. Oh, I know!' she added excitedly. 'I'll be a brilliant detective like Sherlock Holmes and solve unsolvable cases!'

'If you can solve them, then technically, they're not unsolvable,' said Priya.

'Ah, but that's the challenge, isn't it? Everyone sees a problem, but Sherlock Holmes can solve it in his mind. And then he has to prove it. I like that.'

'Don't be silly, Veena,' said Sangita. 'Everyone knows you'll be a doctor like your mother! Sonali, just write down *doctor* for Veena.'

'What?' said Veena.

'Of course, you'll follow in your mother's footsteps,' said Priya. 'Why wouldn't you? Your mother is well-respected and brilliant. You'll grow up to be just like her.'

'I think I'd rather be Sherlock Holmes,' Veena muttered, folding her arms with a 'hmph'.

'Being a doctor in the play will be better and we'll get a better mark. Sherlock Holmes is silly,' added Sangita firmly.

In the end they convinced Veena to pretend she wanted to be a doctor and it was easier to go along with them than to argue. She could pretend to be a spy or Sherlock Holmes another time. And perhaps she might become a doctor? It was just a silly school group activity, she told herself. In the play she played the role brilliantly. She had watched her mother at the surgery so many times she felt she knew just what to do. And her friends were happy with her.

5

Blood

'Come on, Veena,' said Sonali after school. Sonali was so excited that Veena was coming to her house. They walked home together chatting all the way.

'Do you think Priya really will be Prime Minister one day?' asked Sonali.

'Of course!' said Veena. 'If she says so, who's going to argue with her?' They both laughed.

Sonali didn't live far from school. As soon as the door opened a little dog ran to greet them. Veena giggled as it jumped on her. There were young children running up and down the hallway and a rainbow parrot in a cage screeching.

'Shush, shush, Polly,' said Sonali. 'Sorry, Veena! He always screeches at visitors.'

'Who is that with you, Sonali?' Sonali's mother came from another room. 'Oh, Veena! Welcome! So lovely to see you again. Come through to the kitchen and we'll have a tea party.'

'Yum!' said Veena.

Sonali's mother set out a tray on the round table in the garden. 'Here you go, girls: the best tea set for your tea party.'

On the tray was a teapot made of fine porcelain and decorated with painted roses with matching cups and saucers, and a sugar bowl with sugar cubes and special silver tongs for picking them up and putting them in your tea. It was delightful. Then Sonali's mother brought out plates of sweets rolled in sesame seeds and dripping with sugar syrup.

'Oh, I feel so grown up!' exclaimed Veena picking up her teacup delicately.

'Ooh, me too!' said Sonali. 'It's not often Mummy lets me use the good cups.'

'It does make the tea taste even better, don't you think?'

Sonali nodded in agreement.

It was such a lovely garden. Veena felt so calm there, surrounded by large leafy plants and tropical flowers. It felt as though the city had faded away. Polly had been let out of the cage and was sitting on Sonali's shoulder, showing off his fine coloured feathers.

When Sonali's mother was carefully clearing the table, she asked, 'How are your mother and father, Veena? And your younger brother?'

'Ashu!' Veena cried. 'I forgot I was supposed to pick up my little brother!'

Thanking Sonali and her mother, Veena ran out of the house and back to the school gate. Her mother was standing there, looking at her watch. At her side was Ashu. Veena was so relieved!

'Mummy, I'm so sorry! I went to Sonali's house and forgot Ashu!'

'I was worried when you didn't come to the surgery. Fortunately, Ashu stayed at school and didn't wander off!'

'I know. Clever boy, Ashu! That was the right thing to do!'

Veena's mother was still quite cross and said, 'Well, hurry up. I have to get back to work.' And she started to walk ahead of them.

Ashu grabbed Veena's hand. 'Did you forget me, Veena?' he asked.

'Well, only temporarily. I mean, I remembered you in the end,' she said. 'How could I ever forget you?' She gave his hand a squeeze. 'You're my favourite brother, after all!'

'Um, I'm you're only brother.'

'Yes, that's also true,' said Veena.

At the surgery Veena sat on a chair reading a book while Ashu played with blocks at her feet. He built a big city with towers and was driving a toy car around them. The room hummed with phones ringing and low chatter. Occasionally, Veena looked from her book to her brother to check on him. She still felt guilty for forgetting him.

Suddenly, a man burst in holding in his arms a child around eight years old, whose leg was gushing blood.

'Help! Quickly, help! My son! I need the doctor now!' he shouted. Veena heard the blocks collapsing as Ashu jumped up. She rubbed his arm to reassure him it would be all right, although she could see blood dripping from the boy's leg onto the floor. Her mother ran into the room and ushered them into her surgery, with Devika's help. For Veena, it felt as if everything was in slow motion. Her eyes blurred, her stomach churned and she felt lightheaded. Then she saw black before her eyes.

Veena opened her eyes, blinking at the light. She was on the floor surrounded by blocks and Devika was standing over her fanning her with the Sherlock Holmes book.

'What happened?' she asked.

'You fainted, Veena. Can I get you a glass of water?' asked Devika. 'You look very pale.'

Veena sat up straight on the chair. 'Yes, please. Water would be lovely.'

'What happened to the boy?' she asked Ashu.

'Mummy came out and didn't even blink. She took them into the surgery and is fixing him.'

Veena smiled and sipped the water, feeling better with every drop. By the time the glass was empty, the father and son emerged from her mother's surgery.

The boy was now in a little wheelchair and his father was smiling. The boy's leg was bandaged and he looked completely calm, his tears all dried up. Veena observed her mother telling them to come back in a week to check the wound and the stitches. They smiled at the doctor before leaving and waved to everyone in the waiting room.

Veena's mother came over to her then and stroked her forehead.

'Are you all right, dear?' she asked. 'Devika said you fainted!'

'Yes, I'm fine now, Mummy. I think it was the blood. I saw it dripping and then I felt dizzy … and that was the last thing I remember.'

'That sometimes happens for people,' said her mother with a frown.

'But it doesn't happen to you?' asked Veena.

'No, seeing blood has never bothered me,' her mother answered.

'Mummy, I'm sorry I forgot Ashu after school,' Veena said.

'It's fine. It's lovely that you went to see your school friend. Just make sure you let Devika or me know what you're doing.'

After dinner that night, Veena's father was looking everywhere for something he had lost. He was searching through the kitchen drawers, his pockets and briefcase.

'Has anyone seen my good ballpoint pen?' asked her father.

'Um, you mean this one?'

Veena tipped out what was in her pockets onto the kitchen table – it was the ballpoint pen in pieces.

'Is that my best work pen?' her father asked.

'Yes, it's a good pen. It's so good that I wanted to see how it worked,' Veena said.

'I see,' said her father, sitting down at the table with her.

'And so I took it apart,' continued Veena.

Her father ruffled her hair and asked, 'And what have you discovered?'

She showed him all the pieces: spring cartridge, nib, case and clicking stem.

'Do you think you can put it back together again?' he asked her.

'I think so,' Veena replied.

She carefully balanced the nib into the barrel case followed by the ink cartridge, the clicker, and the top, and screwed the pieces together at the middle.

'Now try it,' said her father.

Veena clicked the top to activate the nib but the stem slipped and nothing happened. The clicker didn't work.

'Why do you think that has happened?' her father asked.

She looked at the table and there was the spring. She had forgotten to put the spring back in the top to activate the clicker that pushed the nib in and out and allowed the pen to work. Her eyes lit up and she smiled at her daddy.

'The spring. I forgot the spring. Hang on, it will be right in a minute!'

Her nimble fingers unscrewed the pen and pulled the pieces out, then reassembled it with the spring in place.

'Try it now,' said her father.

Click! Click!

'It works!' she said happily.

'And just as well. It's my favourite pen.'

'Here you go, Daddy,' said Veena.

'No, you keep it, Veena.'

'Really?'

'Of course,' he replied.

Veena carefully placed the pen in her top pocket, the way her father always did. He always had a pen in his shirt pocket.

'Now, what else can I take apart?' Veena said cheekily.

'I suggest you experiment on your own toys from now on!' laughed her father.

'Well, maybe not my toys,' said Veena and then her eyes lit up, 'but Ashu's toys would do very well!'

That night as Veena was trying to sleep, as soon as she closed her eyes she kept seeing the boy with the bleeding leg. She got up and went to the kitchen to get a drink of water.

'Are you alright, Veena?' asked her mother.

'I keep seeing that boy when I close my eyes.'

'Seeing blood like that can take quite a bit of getting used to for some people,' her mother explained.

She gave her mother a hug and went back to bed. Even though she hadn't played with her doll for years, she got her down from the shelf. The doll who had been with her for almost as long as she could remember. Holding her now instantly made Veena feel less lonely.

'I don't think I want to be a doctor if I have to deal with that,' she said to the doll. Veena thought about her mother's job. She knew her mother could heal people and change their lives for the better. That part of being a doctor she would like. That was something Veena aspired to do. *That's it,* she thought. *No matter what I do, I want to change lives for the better.*

6

Treasure collector

'You're up early,' Veena's mother said. Veena was in the kitchen getting some water and the sun wasn't even up yet. 'Do you want to come with me to collect the milk?'

'Yes, please!'

It wasn't every day that Veena's mother went out to collect the milk. It was something special and fun being out in the city as it woke up, stretched, and got going. Outside, the streets were already sizzling with activity and the market stalls were opening for business. The city of Mumbai really was a city that never slept.

Veena and her mother joined the foot traffic in the early glow of dawn. Even though she was now twelve years old, Veena had to walk fast to keep up with her. She could hear the gentle chink of the empty milk bottles her mother carried in a bag on her shoulder.

When they arrived there was already a queue of people. They were holding all sorts of vessels – earthenware jugs, metal canisters – ready to fill them with fresh milk, cream, yoghurt, and butter. Veena noticed how people re-used plastic and glass containers and bottles for refilling, including her mother who handed over the washed milk bottles to be filled. Afterwards, on the way home, they slowed down a little and wandered the streets.

Having her mother all to herself was special for Veena. They meandered through market stalls enjoying the mouth-watering aroma of fresh roti baking on large flat round hotplates called *tavas*, along with bhaji and spicy dahls. The cooks all worked expertly and fast, dishing out breakfast to the crowds already milling about.

'I think it's time for breakfast!' her mother declared.

They ordered cups of sweet spicy chai tea and steamed rice cakes called *idlis*, then sat down at a little table that Veena could see was made from a recycled tea chest. The seats were simply milk crates with cushions. The people in her city were so inventive.

'Getting the milk reminds me of our holidays with Bhuaji,' Veena said.

Bhuaji was her grandfather and he lived in Dehli, the capital of India. In India, a grandfather on your mother's side was usually called **Nanaji** but Bhuaji wasn't like other grandfathers, so it seemed

Nanaji means grandfather in India. It is the name for the maternal father, your mother's father.
Naniji is the name for grandmother on your mother's side, your mother's mother.
The name for the grandparents on your father's side are different.
Dadaji is the name for your paternal grandfather, your father's father.
Dadiji is the name for your paternal grandmother.
The suffix 'ji' on the end of a name is a sign of respect and affection.

right that he would have a different name. He was a dynamic person, very energetic like Veena and her mother. He also would go out early to get the milk every day. Veena loved going with him when they stayed at his house.

'Even when I was a girl, Bhuaji went out in the morning to collect the milk before he went to work in the office. I used to go with him,' said her mother.

'Is that why you always like getting up early?' asked Veena

'I suppose so. It's what I've always done. You get more done in your day with those few extra hours!'

Breakfast at the market stall was delicious. 'Should we take some home to Daddy and Ashu?' asked Veena. 'Good thinking!' said her mother.

*

Now that she was older, Veena no longer had to look after her brother or go to her mother's surgery after school. In fact, she could go to a friend's house or just go home. But what she liked to do most was to go into the poorer parts of the city where so much was happening – food stalls, market stalls, washing draped on ropes overhead and people everywhere.

She would wander through the streets of Mumbai, losing herself in the noise and movement. Some areas were piled high with rubbish and children were fetching out the glass bottles and cans.

'What are you doing?' she asked them.

A girl handed her a hessian sack. 'Here! Take this. Collect up the bottles and cans, too. We take them to the recycling plant and get money.'

Veena found this was like an adventure. She looked through the rubbish seeking treasure. When she found a glass bottle or aluminium can, she put it in her sack as the girl had told her. She wandered the streets mesmerised by the search and delighted when she found something.

'Come on!' said the girl. 'I'll show you where we take them.'

She went with the girl, all the while wondering what might be made from the bottles. Are they turned into telescope lenses? Fancy snow domes? Glass eyes for a pirate?

When she handed over the sack, the young man counted how many glasses and cans she had collected. 'Excuse me,' Veena asked. 'But what do you make the bottles into when you recycle them?'

'What do you mean?' the man answered. 'The bottles are made into more bottles and the cans are made into more cans.'

'Oh,' said Veena. She was a bit disappointed; it was that basic. Surely things could be recycled into something better than what they were?

'Here is your money,' he said, handing over five rupee (around nine cents) for each piece collected. Veena couldn't believe how easy that was! There is value in rubbish. She grasped her earnings in her hand all the way home, and decided she liked being a recycling worker.

On her way home that day, she saw some boys sitting on the ground with a pile of old televisions and radios. Looking closer, she could see that they were taking the devices apart, stripping them of wires and parts and putting the pieces into boxes. Behind them, men were using the parts for repairs and replacements. That's when she noticed the recycling ingenuity all around her. **Ghee** tins being used for growing vegetables, a suitcase turned into a cupboard, a man resoling shoes, a shopping bag made from flour sacks, a mat from carefully folded sweets wrappers woven together. These people were so ingenious. She had heard the phrase that 'necessity is the mother of invention' and here she saw invention all around her. She saw how there was value in all the rubbish if people were clever enough to see that value.

There's a lot of rubbish lying around that ends up polluting the environment, Veena thought. *I wonder how I could improve things for these people around me?* She knew she didn't have the answers, but her heart was telling her it was important and that perhaps, one day, she would be able to help.

7

High school

Veena was late home, yet again, after exploring the slum areas and collecting more rubbish and peering into factories at the machinery, wondering how everything worked.

'Where have you been?' asked her mother. 'I need to pin up this hem.' Her mother was in the middle of making Veena a new outfit. She was growing quite fast and was at high school now. Veena desperately wanted a fashionable denim skirt. Her mother pushed down the foot pedal and the sewing machine whirred along, the needle going up and down, connecting the fabric with a neat straight white stitch.

'Oh, is that my denim skirt?' exclaimed Veena excitedly.

'Yes, and look, I've made you a lovely red top to wear with it.'

Next to the machine was a little box containing extra bobbins and needles, oil and cleaning brushes and a tiny screwdriver. Veena held the screwdriver up to the light.

'No, Veena! No taking apart my sewing machine!' said her mother, continuing to sew. Veena was surprised. Her mother hadn't even looked up from the sewing. She must have eyes in the back of her head!

'How did you know what I was thinking?' asked Veena with folded arms.

Her mother just smiled. 'Here, try this on so I can see the length.'

Veena put on the red shirt and denim skirt while her mother carefully pinned up the hem to a good length, just at her knee. The skirt and top were perfect. But for Veena, there was something missing from the outfit.

'A pocket! I need a pocket! Somewhere for my pen and for the money from collecting the recycling.'

'Hmm,' said her mother. 'I think you're right. I have just the thing.'

Veena's mother went to her sewing basket and found her old dress. It was a bright swirly paisley print with two small pockets on the front, one of which she carefully unpicked.

'What about this?'

Her mother pinned the pocket carefully to the top.

'Perfect! Thank you, Mummy.' Veena felt very grown up in this outfit.

That night Veena used the little sewing machine screwdriver to take apart Ashu's toy train and put it back together again. It was a handy little screwdriver and would fit perfectly in her new pocket.

Next day Veena brushed her wild, curly hair and put on her school uniform – a navy pleated skirt with a clean white shirt and tie. She always started the day neat and tidy. She smiled happily at herself in the mirror and went off to school. Her high school was only for girls and she had many friends.

At lunchtime she was with her friends when a teacher walked past and exclaimed, 'Veena Sahajwalla, tidy yourself up!'

Her friends laughed as she quickly tucked her shirt back in and patted down her hair.

'You're always so dishevelled by lunchtime,' said Geeta.

'I know!' Veena said, exasperated. 'I don't even realise it's happening. I'm just busy learning!'

Veena would be so engrossed in her lessons that by lunchtime her fingers would be marked with blue ink, her tie loose and her shirt tails untucked. And as for her hair? It seemed as if all the thoughts, connections and learning that was filling her brain with buzz couldn't be contained and her hair continually broke free of hairclips.

But Veena was not too fussed with the reprimand. Sometimes Geeta told her to do neater work, but that would slow her down. She didn't care about neat – she wanted to absorb as much knowledge as she could as fast as she could.

In her second year of high school, the English class put on a play of the book they were studying – ***Pride and Prejudice***.

There were five sister roles, a mother, and the male characters. Veena didn't mind what role she got but dearly hoped for a big part. She would even happily play the haughty Mr Darcy. In fact, she could hardly contain her excitement. She had never been in a play like this before. The class was full of anticipation when the teacher read out who had got which part. She had already mentioned the sister roles and Mr Darcy as well, and still Veena's name hadn't been mentioned.

'Mrs Bennet will be played by Veena,' the teacher said.

Veena was over the moon! Mrs Bennet! The mother. It was a very dramatic role too, and Veena could really throw herself into it. It also meant she could boss around her friends who would be playing her daughters.

They all got out their scripts and began to read.

'It says here that Mrs Bennet "was a woman of mean undertaking, little information, and uncertain temper",' Veena read aloud to Geeta. 'And listen to this: "when she was discontented, she fancied herself nervous".'

'Well,' said Geeta, 'show us your nervous disposition then!'

Veena flung her hand to her head and cried, 'Oh dear, my poor nerves!' The others all laughed.

It was going to be the best term of English ever. Classes were spent reading, analysing the text and rehearsing. Some days they were even allowed to rehearse outside. It felt so unlike all the other classes that were always serious. To be acting out scenes felt cool and Veena felt rebellious when they were sitting outside and performing their dramatic scenes. But other teachers often thought they were outside because they were being punished. Veena was right in the middle of a dramatic Mrs Bennet monologue when a teacher came up and said, 'Veena Sahajwalla! Why are you carrying on like that!'

'What do you mean? We're rehearsing our play!'

'Oh, well, that's all right then,' said the teacher. 'Just keep the noise down!'

'Why me?' Veena said to Geeta after the teacher left. 'Why do the teachers always think I'm up to something?'

'I think it's your cheeky smile,' said Geeta.

'Oh, my nerves! You take delight in vexing me! My poor nerves!' she answered in her best Mrs Bennet voice.

The opening night of *Pride and Prejudice* finally came around. Costumes were ready, the 19th-century dresses and frock coats, top hats and bonnets. Backstage was a flurry of excitement.

Veena had never done anything like this before. When the curtain opened and the play began, all jitters were gone and the girls all worked together to see the culmination of their rehearsals come to fruition.

Everything ran perfectly, ending with the appreciative applause from the audience. It was such an achievement to work together and put on a play. Veena's Mrs Bennet was legendary, a hilarious, highly strung, and dramatic performance. Even though she enjoyed treading the boards as an actor, she found the performance equally exhilarating and exhausting. She would never forget taking her bow and hearing the applause.

8

Dissecting frogs

Veena walked to the bus stop after school, swinging her school bag onto her shoulder full of books to take home and do her homework. She didn't find homework annoying. She enjoyed feeling the power of knowledge propelling her into her future. Some extra work always interested her. Which is why her bag was so heavy!

Veena changed schools for the final two years of high school. Her new school was co-ed and had a specialist focus on science, which had become her passion. When she enrolled, her mother said, 'Hey, you love science, which is great. Have you thought about going into medicine?'

Veena knew that medicine was the obvious pathway for most girls who were good at science. But she pulled a face and said, 'I can't deal with thinking about that yet!'

'Well, you'll have to think about university soon enough!' said her mother.

The atmosphere at the new school was ambitious, studious and energetic. Everyone focusing on the final two years of high school, already knowing they were on the way to careers in science.

In biology, the students took their places at the laboratory tables.

'Get into pairs, please,' the teacher instructed. Veena and Geeta grabbed each other immediately. 'Today we will be dissecting a frog,' the teacher continued.

Veena pulled a face.

'It will be fine, Veena,' said Geeta. 'Come on.'

Veena stood next to Geeta, their scalpels ready. The teacher had put instructions on the blackboard and they had a diagram in their textbook open beside them.

'Are you ready?' asked Geeta.

Veena pulled another funny face as a reply and Geeta laughed. Then she took a breath and looked down at the poor dead frog before her. His skin was olive green with spots and still shiny. She poked the flesh through her rubber gloves and checked if the frog was really dead.

The teacher listed all the parts of the frog. 'Note the membrane over the frog's eyes,' she told them. Geeta leaned in closer and delicately slipped her tweezers between the eye and the membrane.

'Interesting,' she said.

'Hmm,' agreed Veena watching.

'Now look inside the frog's mouth,' the teacher said, and Geeta did this showing Veena where the tongue connected. Veena made approving, fascinated noises but looked away while the teacher continued.

'Now flip the frog onto its back and expose the smooth belly. Make an incision into the skin at the base of the back leg.'

'Here goes,' Geeta declared, and made the first slice with the scalpel. She pulled the skin off like a sock, exposing the leg muscles. She breathed a sigh of relief and puffed some air up that flicked her fringe out of her eyes. So far so good.

'The next incision is across the belly,' the teacher instructed.

'Your turn,' said Geeta, handing Veena the scalpel.

Veena told herself she could do this. She tried to make a delicate cut but suddenly liquid oozed out and she uttered a little screech.

'Shush!' laughed Geeta. Veena tried to contain herself, pulling a face to stop herself giggling, but as she went to make another incision the frog squirted out liquid again and Veena couldn't stop laughing. They managed to control themselves, swallowing the laughs and listening to the teacher telling them to cut through to see the frog's internal organs.

Veena looked at Geeta. 'I think you should do this next bit,' she said

'I think you need more practice,' retorted her friend.

Veena sighed and leaned over the frog.

The teacher explained how they would 'see the frog's heart, liver and stomach'.

'Here goes,' Veena said, as she made the next incision. But she sliced too deeply and all she could see was a gooey mess.

'Hmm,' Geeta said. 'Remind me not to let you operate on me when you're a doctor!'

'I don't think I'm going to be a doctor,' Veena said, starting to giggle again.

Geeta giggled too. Veena composed herself, frowned, concentrated, and ploughed on but only made it worse. The body of the frog was now a mess of tangled organs.

'I don't think you're going to be a cook either,' laughed Geeta.

Veena held up some squished frog on her scalpel. 'Mmm, yummy! **Tandoori** frog!'

Geeta laughed until tears ran down her face.

'Poor frog,' said Veena composing herself just in time to not get into trouble from the teacher.

Later, when she got home and thought about how messy she was at dissecting the frog, it worried her. Would she be a doctor?

'What are you frowning about?' asked Ashu.

'I had to dissect a frog today in biology,' she told him. 'And I wasn't very good at it.'

'Don't worry, you just need practice,' Ashu assured her as he walked out the door.

By the time Ashu came back, their mother was home and Veena was setting the table for dinner. Ashu placed a jar on the table in front of her.

'There you go!' he said. 'Some frogs for you!'

'What is this?' asked their mother. 'What is a jar of frogs doing on the dinner table? Ashu?'

'Veena had to dissect a frog today at school and she said she failed so I thought she might need to practise!'

'It's true, Mummy,' added Veena. 'Today at school I dissected a frog and it was a disaster! I made such a mess.'

Her mother laughed.

'You know, with a bit of practice you get better at things like that,' she said. 'You can always practise and improve.'

'Told you, Veena!' said Ashu.

Veena nodded thoughtfully and frowned.

'Mummy, would you mind if I didn't become a doctor?'

Veena's mother stopped preparing dinner and looked at her daughter.

'What's that?'

She sat with her mother at the kitchen table. It was rare to see her mother stop and remain still.

'I know you want me to be a doctor, Mummy, but I'm worried that biology isn't my best subject.'

'Of course, I don't mind if you become a doctor or not. The main thing is that whatever you do you do to your best ability. And you have great ability.'

Veena smiled and rested her head on her mother's shoulder. She was so lucky to have supportive parents – her father had always said much the same thing.

'Now, time for me to finish making dinner,' her mother said.

'Thank you for the frogs, Ashu,' said Veena. 'But I don't think I have the stomach for killing them. After dinner let's go downstairs and let them go.'

*

In a later biology experiment, Veena's class dissected a cockroach. The hard body and neatness of the interior were much more appealing to Veena. Less gooey and cleaner. She did much better with it. At home she told her parents.

'We've done a lot of practice dissecting frogs but I got a cockroach for the test today and I actually found it a lot neater and clean. Very organised and systematic whereas with a frog it is always so messy. I liked the cockroach better.'

'Hmm, yes, more like machinery,' her father remarked.

'That's right,' said Veena. 'Like an engine. I like machines, actually,' she added.

'Perhaps you could go into **engineering**,' said her father looking over at her mother.

Engineering is the science of applying knowledge of pure sciences, such as physics and chemistry, to design or develop structures, machines, apparatus, or manufacturing processes.

They could both see her natural inclination towards engineering, but both parents knew this was a male-dominated profession, unlike medicine.

'Yes, I've been thinking about that,' she said. 'A lot of the boys at school want to study engineering.'

She waited for her parents to say something about how not many girls do engineering because she knows this is true.

'Engineering is a good profession,' said her father.

That her parents hadn't suggested she couldn't be an engineer because she was a girl was such a relief. She felt glad to have such open-minded parents who wanted her to fulfil her potential.

9

Exams

Veena continued to study hard and excel at school because now she knew for sure what she wanted to do. She had decided to pursue engineering – but not just anywhere. She aspired to go to the top engineering university in India – the Indian Institute of Technology (IIT) in Kanpur.

Her heart did a cartwheel whenever she thought about it. It was an ambitious dream; IIT had a notoriously difficult entrance requirement. Prospective students from all over India sat several exams over two days and only the top students got a place. Veena would have to study for these exams on top of her final year workload.

And if she did get in? She would have to move so far away from home. She would need to be brave. And attempting to get into the best engineering course in India? She knew her family would play an important role in encouraging her, so as soon as the idea crystallised in her mind, she decided she had to tell them.

'Mummy, Daddy,' she said one evening, 'I want to talk to you about university.'

'Oh, lovely,' said her father rubbing his hands with glee. He was so proud of his daughter and knew her future was bright. Veena smiled her wide smile at him. She wanted to please them. She also knew that deep down, her mother still thought Veena would have a career in medicine. Wanting to study engineering was such a big deal when growing up in India – and that was for boys. It was even more of a big deal for a girl. She knew they may not agree with her choice of university – especially wanting to go so far from home. And what if her parents didn't think she was capable of getting into such a prestigious university course?

'I've been looking at my options,' began Veena.

'Yes, as long as you get good marks your options will be open to you,' said her father.

'There are many good places to study at right here in Mumbai,' said her mother.

'Well, the thing is, as you know, I want to study engineering, so I want to sit the entrance exam for IIT,' Veena stated with confidence.

Indian Institute of Technology or IIT is located in Kanpur. It is a technical and research university and was established in 1959 with strong international connections, especially with the USA.

'Oh, but that's so far away!' cried her mother. 'It's over 1000 kilometres from here, Veena!'

'But it's the very best place to study engineering. And if I want to get the best education then I will have to leave home,' said Veena.

'You will only be able to come home in semester break!' pointed out her father. 'We would barely see you!'

'But that's what I want to do.'

Her parents were quiet but nodded their heads in agreement.

'That's if I get in,' continued Veena. 'The entrance exams are extremely hard and hugely competitive.'

Here her parents became enthusiastic.

'Of course, you'll pass the exams,' said her father. 'You'll study hard and prepare well and you'll pass with flying colours!'

'Yes,' agreed her mother. 'You always do your very best and work hard.'

'We'll help you in any way we can,' added her father, putting his arm around her shoulders. 'We have all the faith in the world that if you put your mind to it, you'll achieve it.'

*

The bus was overcrowded, as it was every day. Veena could never get a seat. Instead, she was squashed into the aisle like a sardine, swaying and rocking as she went to and from school. Sometimes she wished she could use this time for extra study but getting a seat and having room to open her bag and get out her books would be like winning the lottery. What this time *was* good for, however, was daydreaming. As the bus lurched, Veena adjusted her balance and let her mind wander.

When she alighted from the bus to go home, she saw her friend, Panna, just in front of her. The bus had been so crowded that she hadn't seen her until now. Panna went to a different school but lived in the same apartment building as Veena.

'Panna!' she called.

She ran to catch up and the two girls fell into step with each other.

'How are you?' asked Panna. 'I haven't seen you for ages.'

'I'm well, you know, studying hard,' Veena answered.

'Oh, yes, me too. I really want to get good marks,' said Panna.

'Do you know what university you want to study at?'

'I haven't decided yet. What about you?'

'I've decided I'm going to be an engineer! I want to go to IIT in Kanpur,'

'No way!' exclaimed Panna, impressed. 'That's amazing! Can I tell you a secret?'

'Of course.'

'I want to study engineering too. But I know not many girls do that.'

'We're rare, that's for sure. Why don't you study for the IIT entrance exams too?'

'Me? Go to IIT? I don't know...'

'We can study together! Help each other out!'

'Alright,' said Panna. 'I can't believe I'm saying this. But, yes. I'll do it too. It'd be a dream to go to IIT.'

'Shall I come to your house now and show you a practice exam I just bought?'

Panna nodded and smiled. Veena's enthusiasm was infectious. If they got into IIT they would have the world of innovation and engineering at their feet. And surely two heads were better than one?

Veena looked out Panna's window at the buildings, traffic and whirl of Mumbai. She thought about how engineering could influence *how* we live through *how* we make the world. It was exciting and made her feel as if her hair was standing on end. She put her hand up to her head to make sure her hair, now cut into a shorter style, really wasn't sticking straight up from her head.

At the table Panna and Veena looked over the practice exam. Panna flicked through the booklet, every page covered with complicated equations.

'I don't even know what some of this is,' said Panna.

'Me neither,' confessed Veena. 'But I have my textbooks here. We can work it out. For me, passing these exams is more important than my end of year score.'

'If we get into IIT then our other marks don't really matter,' agreed Panna.

'That's right,' said Veena. 'We'll already have our ticket to our future.'

'This is going to be hard,' said Panna. 'Four exams in two days – chemistry, maths, physics and English.'

'Intense,' agreed Veena. And then she added, 'It's rather thrilling!'

They both smiled and got to work.

They studied together, doing old exams, buying and sharing mock exams, working through the

pages of problems, searching their textbooks – sharing knowledge and helping each other when they got stuck. Between the two of them they could accomplish most of the problems or could work out a plan of attack with each question.

'Hello, Veena,' said Panna's mother, arriving just as Veena was packing up her books to leave. 'Studying together again?'

'Well, we have a lot of work to do for the—'

Panna bumped Veena's arm and she dropped all of her books. They bent down to pick them up and Panna locked eyes with Veena and slightly shook her head to warn her from saying anything more. Veena frowned. When she stood up she said, 'Oh, I'm so clumsy!'

'You girls work too hard,' said Panna's mother. 'You're young girls. You should be having fun too!'

'Studying is fun, Mummy,' said Panna.

After she left, Veena thought about how Panna's mother was the total opposite of her own. It seemed as if she didn't want Panna to study hard and succeed.

As the exams got closer, Panna and Veena's lives got busier with school and family commitments so they didn't even manage to see each other right before the exam days. They had both knuckled down separately for the final push with revision. Veena wasn't sure which exam centre Panna had booked in for as it was held in various places because so many students applied. Just thinking about that reminded her how competitive it was to get a place at IIT.

Finally, the morning of the first exam arrived. Veena was a bundle of emotions. In her head she thought of the character of Mrs Bennet she had played in the school production. '*Oh, my poor nerves!*' she thought to herself and laughed. She was ready. She had studied hard and now she had to put it all into practice over the hours of the exam. Her family warmly wished her luck as she left for the bus.

'Do your best, Veena!' said her mother.

'We know you can do this,' said her father.

'You can do it, Veena. You're my cleverest sister,' said Ashu and smiled.

'I'm your only sister, Ashu,' said Veena laughing.

'Yes, that too,' agreed Ashu, giving her a hug.

As she arrived at the hall where the exam was being held, hundreds of teenagers were already streaming up the steps to the entrance. Veena couldn't help but notice that there were hardly any girls. She did a quick check for Panna but couldn't see her. She told herself to concentrate on the exam now. She would catch up with Panna after it was finished.

The hall echoed with chairs scraping back while the students sat down at the desks set out in rows. Down each side were long rectangular windows; morning light cast stripes over the room. Veena found her place and got out her pencils, pens, calculator and eraser. Her hands fumbled the pencils, and she watched the clock as she listened to the supervisor instructing them all on the rules. This was it. She took a deep breath.

'You can open your booklet now,' announced the exam supervisor.

And Veena did.

Head down and concentrating, tackling each question, remembering formulas and strategies for different equations, Veena was in the moment. The sound of exam supervisors pacing around the room up and down between the desks was like the ticking of the clock. When she came to the end of a page she would look up and check the time. She had to pace herself and not get too preoccupied with problems if they were challenging her. In that way, the three-and-a-half hours passed, until she was finished.

'Pens down.'

There was a collective sigh from the students as they closed their booklets. She had got through it with time to check it over. The first exam was done. Nothing could change that. She would have a break and something to eat before the afternoon exam. It was going to be two days' hard slog to get through.

The next day, Veena had to sit two more exams. She was less nervous now, being more familiar with the surroundings and the process. And she also found she quite enjoyed the challenge! Then finally, it was over. The next part was even harder for her – waiting for months for the letter to arrive to tell her the results.

That evening Veena went to see Panna at her home. She knocked on her bedroom door before bursting in.

'Oh, my gosh! What did you think?' Veena asked.

'Veena, I hope you won't be too disappointed, but I didn't take the exams,' said Panna.

'What? Were you sick? What happened?'

'I'm not like you. I'm not brave. I'm scared to go to IIT all the way in Kanpur. It's so far away. And I'm not even sure my family would allow me.'

Veena was totally shocked. They had worked so hard for this! She couldn't believe Panna didn't go. But she suppressed her surprise and concentrated on being a supportive friend. She sat on Panna's bed with her.

'It's okay, Panna. No big deal,' she said. 'I understand. You'll get excellent marks and have many choices of universities.'

In her heart, though, Veena wondered why Panna didn't do it. It wasn't that she wasn't smart or wasn't prepared. They had studied hard. Veena was disappointed that there wasn't another girl to share her IIT dream with. But also, she didn't want Panna to feel bad.

*

Every day when she arrived home from school Veena checked the letterbox. Would today be the day she would find out her results? And then one day, it was there. The envelope clearly marked with IIT insignia.

She didn't even stop to think before tearing it open. Unfolding the letter, she scanned the words that danced before her eyes. She had passed! She was in! She had been offered a place in the prestigious IIT Engineering degree course. She hugged the letter to her chest and twirled around before running up to the apartment to tell her family.

Her parents were over the moon – although not surprised.

'I knew you could do it!' exclaimed her mother, while her father read the letter out loud over and over.

'Ashu! Can you believe it?' said their father.

'Yes, Daddy, I can,' said Ashu, laughing. 'You've read the letter out loud three times already. I believe it!'

Veena was pinching herself. Her dream of going to IIT to study engineering had come true! She had spent so much time concentrating on the entrance exam for IIT she would now have to catch up on her schoolwork – but knowing she already had her place at university took the pressure off those final end-of-year exams. She had a foot in the door of her future. Now she just had to finish high school.

*

A little time after the school year had finished, Veena arrived home one evening to find her parents waiting for her.

'What's wrong?' she asked.

'Let's go for a walk, Veena,' said her mother.

Her parents accompanied her out onto the street where they fell into an easy stroll together. Veena wondered if she were in trouble.

'What is it, Mummy? Daddy? Is something wrong?' she asked.

Her father pulled out a letter from his pocket. 'Your final marks from school arrived today.'

'Yes?' said Veena wishing he would hand them over.

'Now, you know we love you very much, Veena, and we know how hard you have worked,' said her mother.

'We are very proud,' agreed her father.

Veena was getting worried. They were being so sensitive in their tone, as if they were breaking the news carefully. *Sheesh what happened?* she thought. *I think I've done alright so why are they being so weird?*

'Can you just tell me?'

'Well, here you are,' said her father handing her the letter. 'We don't want you to be upset.'

But Veena wasn't upset. She laughed. She had done very well!

'That's okay! That's good!' Veena said, reading her results.

Veena's parents looked at each other and sighed with relief.

'We thought you might be disappointed,' said her mother. 'We know what a high achiever you are.'

'Disappointed?' cried Veena. 'I'm going to IIT Kanpur to study engineering. I already knew that before my exams. These school results don't really matter, even though I'm glad I have done well. I'm already into a university. The best university in India!'

10

Homesick

The letter from the Indian Institute of Technology had instructed Veena to attend the university to make subject selections before the course started. She couldn't wait to see the place where she would be spending the next four years studying. Feeling so grown up to be embarking on this next step in life, she was not impressed when her father said, 'I will come with you to Kanpur. It's a long way from home.'

'Perhaps I should come too?' said her mother.

'What?!' said Veena. 'Daddy coming will be embarrassing enough! Not both of you, please!'

Please let me not be the only one there with a parent! she thought. She would be mortified if she was, especially if the boys didn't have their parents with them.

Her parent's concern was understandable. Kanpur was over twelve hundred kilometres from home. When the time came, she caught the train with her father. It took a whole night and most of the day to get there and while her father slept, Veena tossed and turned with excitement. She looked out the window at the world flicking by and felt the train wheels click-clacking on the tracks in time with her galloping heart.

The university was as grand as she imagined. Walking around the campus, Veena couldn't wait for the first day. They looked over the laboratories, lecture halls, and classrooms. The campus was modern, multi-storeyed, and spread out over a large area. Veena noted how many bicycles were parked outside each building. It seemed to be the way to get around the large university.

'I think your accommodation is this way,' said her father looking at the map on the brochure.

'No, Daddy, that's the boy's dormitory. The girls' is this way.'

Veena was rubbernecking all over the place, trying to take in the buildings, gain a sense of direction and see the other new students. She was finally at IIT and could not stop smiling as they explored. Of course, Veena was not the only one there with a parent to help them, and fortunately, her father did not embarrass her at all. Looking over the campus, however, she couldn't help but notice that almost everyone was male. When she saw another female student, she would catch her eye and smile. Were there really going to be so few girls studying here?

Her father helped her fill out all the enrolment information and subject selection. The course would begin with two years of general training for all the students in science and maths. Following that, there would be specialisations to choose from, including electrical engineering, civil engineering, metallurgical engineering, and aeronautical engineering. But right now, Veena was only concentrating on the beginning.

*

When it was time to travel to Kanpur to begin first semester, Veena was finally getting her wish to feel like an adult. The reality of leaving her family didn't hit until it was time to say goodbye. Up until then, she was simply excited. Her mother had helped her get some new clothes and pack, and they had been running around getting everything ready.

Hugging Ashu, now taller than her, and looking at her parents, both sadness and pride playing over their faces, the importance of this transition couldn't be denied. She was moving a long way from home and embarking on the next phase of her life alone. And no matter how ready she felt, it was still a jolt for them all.

'I'll be fine, Mummy,' she assured her mother. 'I'll call you when I arrive.'

'I know, I know,' said her mother. 'I know you're going to love it there, Veena, and you'll do so well.'

'I'm so proud of you,' said her father.

*

Arriving at the women's dormitory the next day, she located her room with the help of the campus porters and, after dumping her bags, she found the common room where some other female students were gathered.

'Nice to meet you, Veena,' said a girl by the window. 'I'm Rita. I think I've got the room next to yours.'

Veena smiled her big smile.

'Where are all the other girls?' she asked.

'What other girls? It's just us!' Rita said, indicating the handful of girls in the room.

Veena knew they would be in the minority, but this was much less than a minority.

'Just us?!'

She soon realised just how rare it was for females to be studying engineering. Out of the almost 250 students in that year's intake, there were only ten females. Her mind flew to her study friend, Panna. Knowing how different her family was from her own, Veena thought that perhaps she wouldn't have been allowed to come all this way to study.

University life was a steep learning curve, which Veena loved. She found her way around campus, got to know her timetable, her lecturers' names, how to use the library systems, what to order from the canteen – and what *not* to order! She enjoyed the feeling of being responsible for herself and living away from home. She felt ready and capable. The work was challenging but Veena, as always, threw herself into learning with characteristic determination and curiosity.

On the weekends, the other girls lived close enough to go home to their families.

'See you on Sunday night, Veena,' said Rita standing at Veena's doorway. 'I feel terrible leaving you,' she added.

'Don't be silly! I'd go home, too, if I could!' said Veena putting on a brave face. 'Don't worry about me. I'll have the whole place to myself! Imagine all the study I'll get done with the peace and quiet.'

She would watch them leave, their bags packed and a lightness in their step, knowing they would see their families soon. At first, Veena tried to be positive about being alone on the weekends. Perhaps it would be fun having the whole dormitory to herself? Even the whole dining hall to herself! But sitting alone for dinner wasn't so wonderful and her spirits started sinking to her boots.

'Here, have some extra **gulab jarmun**,' said the lady serving the food, feeling sorry for her.

'Oh, lovely, thank you,' said Veena sadly. 'I love sweet things.'

'Yes, we've noticed,' she replied, and Veena laughed. She already had a reputation for her love of desserts. She sat down alone in the dining hall and ate a spoonful of the spongy syrupy pudding. It was delicious. The sweetness coated her mouth and cheered her a little.

It was on these lonely weekends when Veena's homesickness was at its most intense. She would use the communal payphone in the female dormitory to call home. Not wanting to worry her family, she pretended to be fine at first. But soon her conversations with her family back in Mumbai were punctuated with tears and sobs.

Homesickness was an ailment even her mother couldn't cure, although she did try. Her mother would distract her by talking about what Veena loved – her studies!

'Tell me again about that lab experiment,' she would say and, 'What's the assignment you're working on?'

This would remind Veena why she was there in the first place. To learn. And it would also remind her that she was at the best university in India for engineering.

Although Veena loved the study and the classes, the years at university were hard. Many, many times she thought, *Why am I doing this? I could get into any engineering course and live at home or transfer somewhere else. Is this really worth it?*

But she carried on.

Being in the minority sometimes made her angry, too, especially when she saw that there were different rules for the male students compared to the female students. For instance, the male dormitory had a 24-hour canteen, whereas theirs was only open for a few hours; and the female students had a curfew, meaning they could not leave their dormitory after 9 p.m. And she saw the way the boys dominated class discussions, refused to share data and lab results for group assignments, and walked around the university as if they owned the place.

So much was not fair.

One night the girls were up late studying, well past curfew, books spread out on the common room floor.

'Has anyone got any snacks?' Veena asked.

Everyone shrugged and admitted they didn't.

'This is impossible,' Veena exclaimed. 'If we stay up late like this, we need a midnight feast.'

'Sorry, Veena,' said Rita. 'I didn't really get organised.'

'It's okay,' said Veena. 'I know where I can get food. Wait here.'

'But what about curfew?'

Veena just laughed and said, 'They can try and catch me, but I'll be so stealthy, they won't even know what's happened.'

It was dark. Veena got on her bicycle and rode under the moonlight to the canteen in the male dormitory. She hid her bike in the bushes and peeked through the window. There were only a few male students in there. She watched as they grabbed their snacks and left. It was now or never. She ran in and stuffed her bag with chips, chocolates and biscuits. Hearing voices, she dashed out of there as fast as she could, retrieved her bicycle and pedalled off.

'Hey, you!' she heard a man shout. But she was too fast and rode back at full speed.

Out of breath but triumphant, she burst into the room. The others cheered and clapped as Veena tipped the bag of snacks onto the floor.

'Midnight feast, anyone?' she said with a flourish.

Veena hated the inequality between the male students and the female students. *That's another thing I'm going to change,* she thought. *I'm going to change the image of scientists as being a man in a white lab coat. I'll show the world that women can be scientists too.*

*

Each year Veena would return home to Mumbai for the summer break. It was always such a relief to be back with her family. The whole summer she would feel at ease, comforted by the presence of her family where she would relax and enjoy herself. Then all of a sudden summer would be over, and it would be time to return to Kanpur.

Leading up to catching the train back to university, Veena would become so sad.

'Be strong,' her mother would say. 'Tell me about the subjects you'll be doing this semester.'

That's how her mother always helped her to stay positive, reminding her to keep looking forward. Veena's homesickness would peak immediately after she returned to university. Then slowly she would become absorbed in her studies and homesickness would be kept at bay.

11

Odd one out

Two years into her studies it was time to specialise. The ten girls in her year were divided up into even smaller groups with some of them choosing electrical engineering, others chemical engineering, and the remainder, civil engineering. Veena chose to specialise in metallurgical engineering, which looked at how different metals are made. She was the only girl who did.

One of the things that always fascinated Veena about metals was the way they could be made into different shapes She was enthralled with the transformation of these materials through the power of fire. It was a kind of magic.

When Veena entered the lecture theatre for the first lecture and sat down, the male students came in and sat in the row in front and the row behind her – nobody sat in the same row as her.

Okay, so what? she thought. As each boy found his place and she realised she would be sitting completely on her own, it stung. Not only would they not sit next to her, but they also wouldn't even sit in the same row? It was hard not to take this to heart, no matter how strong she was. But in the end Veena knew she had to turn this into a positive too.

Yep, that's cool, she thought. *If I'm going to be sitting on my own, then I may as well get the best seat.* And with that thought she decided to sit in the first row on her own, focus on the lecture and get the most out of every single lecture and class. If the boys wouldn't be her friends, then she would have to make friends with the lecturers and talk to them about her passion for metal processing. Some lecturers recognised how Veena was feeling and would encourage her to chat after class; and being in the front row meant she was always first in line to see the lecturer and ask questions.

Nevertheless, the sense of isolation was acute. She no longer had other girls she could study or discuss lectures with and the male students refused to talk to her. Sometimes when she was studying, she would find she was talking to herself, including celebrating **Eureka moments** when she finally understood a knotty problem. Then she would think, *I need to take a break! I'm talking to myself! Isn't that the first sign of madness?*

Often, she would walk to the local store during these breaks to buy a snack as well as a few sweet treats to get her through the next study period. At the counter she would find herself talking to the shop owner about what she had been studying that day – heat transfer in metal processing, maybe.

'I realised today, and it was so fascinating...' she began. She talked in **Hindi** but all the technical jargon was in English. She would be so excited by what she was learning that she just *had* to talk about it to someone. The shop owner always listened with respect and interest.

Hindi is the language of northern India, derived from the ancient language, Sanskrit. It is the fourth most widely spoken language in the world, with more than 250 million people speaking it as their first language.

'You're so clever,' he would say. 'I think you are going to be a famous scientist one day.'

Veena would laugh. 'Thanks for listening. I'll see you soon.'

*

When homesickness overwhelmed her now, Veena had learnt to concentrate on the positives. The canteen staff knew she was alone on the weekends and gave her as much food as she wanted. 'Here, have seconds,' they would say. Still, sometimes she used to wonder: *Why am I doing this? It's so hard.*

Worst of all was when she needed the male students in her class to share the group laboratory data for big lab reports, they would exclude her. What could she do? In the end, the unfairness only made her bolder. She knew she had put in the hard work and deserved to do well. There was no way she was going to be stopped by her fellow students. She would find a way to get her work done.

So, under the moonlight, Veena rode her bicycle around Kanpur to visit her lecturers, to get the information she needed.

One thing that kept her interested in that lonely third year of her course was the prospect of her summer holiday work placement. She had organised to do a hot metal internship in Mumbai, where she would be up close with the transformation of metals. While not quite on an industrial scale, the internship would see Veena working in factories and seeing red hot smelting on a much bigger scale than in the laboratory at university. This is where she could finally see how metallurgical engineering worked in the real world.

She was so pleased when once again she was on semester break and home with her family in Mumbai. On her first day of her internship, she rose early with her mother and got ready. Her mother had not slowed down one bit and was still hard to keep up with.

'Okay, I'm heading off to work now,' declared Veena, as she grabbed her satchel to walk out the door.

'Hang on, hang on! Wait for me!' said her father. 'I'll accompany you there.'

'Are you serious, Daddy? I've lived in the city all my life. I've lived out of home for years now. Do you really think I need to be chaperoned there?'

'I know you are a capable woman, Veena, but I would feel better if I took you there myself,' he answered.

Veena smiled and sighed. She was happy to be back at home, even if she did find her parents overprotective.

'How about you walk me to the bus stop?' she suggested.

'Just to the bus stop? Okay, okay,' agreed her father.

They walked together. Veena loved being back in her beloved, wild, chaotic city. She couldn't wait to be part of the factory life that was at the heart of the city's manufacturing.

'Okay, Daddy, we are here now. I'll see you tonight,' she said, when they arrived at the bus stop.

But her father made no move to leave.

'I'll just wait with you for the bus,' he said.

Veena raised her eyebrows at him as if to say, 'Really?'

'Come on, Veena,' he said. 'Indulge your father a little. I've missed you.'

Veena smiled. She had missed her family too.

The bus arrived and Veena pushed her way on. When she looked out the window, she saw her father waving until he was out of sight.

Veena was excited to see how the factory operated. The machinery, the manufacturing and how the metal was transformed and moulded into shapes. It was a noisy, busy day but it was exhilarating to see red hot steel, with enough force applied, converted into another shape. You don't have to be a scientist to be mesmerised by the process of transformation and the joy of seeing how things are made; but with her scientific interest as well, the whole experience was mind-blowing.

Summer wore on and Veena became comfortable at home, surrounded by her supportive family

and the love they shared, along with the fun and all the new things she was learning in her internship. She began to dread going back to Kanpur. Recognising the symptoms of homesickness and knowing her daughter so well, her mother began to try and cure them in ways she could. The one thing Veena felt stronger than homesickness was her enthusiasm for learning. And so, the conversations would begin.

'What subjects have you got next semester?' her mother would ask. 'Where are your textbooks? Have you read them yet?' 'Have you made a start on the coursework, Veena? You need a good head start for next semester.'

And Veena would do as her clever doctor mother suggested. In the evenings, she read her textbooks and got excited about the coming semester, occasionally looking up and discussing chapters with her parents. Her mother nodded and smiled and said encouraging things like, 'You're so lucky to be at ITT'. 'You are doing so well.' 'Best university in the country for engineering.' 'My brilliant daughter.'

All of these things buffeted Veena forward like a strong breeze. She tried to look forward, to be enthusiastic about learning and grateful for her good fortune in having an encouraging family. She could do this. She was almost there. And her mother was right – she was lucky to be at such a wonderful university where the opportunities were amazing.

12

Scholarship

One of the opportunities from studying at IIT was that international professors attended conferences and gave lectures or presentations. In Veena's final year, **Professor Brimacombe** visited from Canada. He was a charismatic teacher with a genuine interest in the students. His approach to science and metallurgical engineering was different too. He wasn't only interested in the theo-

Professor Keith Brimacombe was one of the world's leading and most innovative **process metallurgists** of the 20th century, and an outstanding teacher.

retical, he was interested in the practical application of technology and how it could improve industry. Veena instantly connected with his way of thinking.

'Yes, you have to do the theory, the analysis, and the experiments, but alongside that you have to be considering what it means in the real world,' he told the students.

This was grand thinking and Veena liked it. She had always wanted to help people and Professor Brimacombe's approach showed her this was possible in her chosen profession.

When Veena first spoke to him after a class, she was a little starstruck. But the professor was a down-to-earth person who liked a chat and could strike up a conversation easily. She felt so humbled that he would talk to her, but he treated her seriously and engaged with what she had to say. From his visit, Veena confirmed many of her ideas about her future.

'Science is for humanity. That's why we do science,' he said. 'Scientists have the sense of a bigger purpose about humanity.'

Yes! thought Veena. This was what she, too, believed.

He was interested in her work and study and said, 'If you come top of the class, you'll have no problem getting a scholarship to study for your master's at Vancouver.'

Veena was learning about how connections with wonderful people can change the course of your life. This was what it was like to be part of the scientific community. Older scientists mentored younger scientists and were supportive. Rather than the competitive nature of university study, Veena was learning that scientific answers were not developed overnight but rather through a constant journey of improving and learning through a supportive scientific community. Veena wanted to be part of that.

Through this experience Veena realised that encouragement from people who are already working in the field is hugely important to students, and that one day she would like to encourage and mentor young scientists, too.

Already a determined student, Veena gained new motivation. She was impressed with the professor and knew she wanted to continue her studies with him in Canada. Top of the class? Bring it on! Her biggest competitor was Sanjay. They were always first and second in their marks. In fact, as soon as they got a marked assignment back, they would compare their results.

'What did you get on the assignment?' Sanjay would say.

'Why don't you tell me first what you got?' Veena would respond with a cheeky smile.

They would flick through each other's work, seeing where marks were added or dropped, comparing the standard of their own work against the other.

'What are those two talking about?' asked one student watching as they talked intently.

'If they're talking to each other, it's always about marks! Always trying to see who's the best and who has done better.'

Although it was mostly a healthy competition, at times it was intense. Veena felt disadvantaged because the male students all lived in the same hostel, having meals together and discussing assignments. She wished there was at least one other girl in her class to share with. But there wasn't, so she had to work with what she had. While the lecturers gave her support, she had to find the determination and discipline to study –

hard and long. Now she had added motivation as well. She really wanted that scholarship to study in Vancouver with Professor Brimacombe.

Before the end of the course, the entire class went on an industrial site visit in southern India. It was a big excursion, travelling almost the length of India for a chance to see an actual steel plant. It was Veena's first major trip away from home apart from being at university. The class was excited to go, knowing this was a look at the next phase in their lives after graduating. This was about applying what they were learning in the real world – a taste of what the future might hold. Veena took in every detail.

She knew that to create steel, iron ore is heated in a blast furnace up to around 1,500 degrees Celsius with a type of coal called coke. But now she was witnessing the transformation! She was entranced.

After the exams, which marked the end of the year and her engineering degree, there was a month before graduation. Veena went home, but through those weeks, she was totally convinced Sanjay would be ranked first in metallurgical engineering. He had the peer support, lab reports, friendships, a group working together with him. Veena applied for many universities to study for her master's, while secretly hoping for that scholarship to Canada.

Her family came with her when she went back to Kanpur for her graduation. Wearing her flowing graduation gown, she walked up on stage to receive her graduation certificate. Then she was handed a second certificate. She had graduated top of the class! She looked over to Sanjay and his friends and held up her two certificates in triumph. She had done it! Now her dreams could come true.

*

Going to Canada was another brave step for Veena, but that showed the power of one human being to inspire others. Veena knew she wanted to study with Professor Brimacombe. Having uplifting and supportive people in her life was so important and she knew this was a fundamental human quality she hoped to share with others too. She was heading off to study a Master of Science in Metals and Materials Engineering at the University of British Columbia. It was going to be an amazing adventure!

‘That’s it,’ said her mother, sitting on her bed. ‘Now that you’re leaving home you’ll never come back to live here again.’

They had been shopping for clothes and got some warm things made. It was hard to imagine a cold place like Vancouver while shopping in the heat of Mumbai. Veena assured her mother that she would return. Of course, she would. Mumbai was her home. But her mother just shook her head and said, ‘You are an adult now. This is your future. And I can see you’re destined for big things beyond Mumbai.’

Veena looked around her room, still the same as when she left it to go to IIT in Kanpur. Her suitcase was packed at her feet. She took her doll down from the shelf. Why had she kept it all this time? But even now, looking at the doll’s face, Veena felt as if she was looking at a friend. ‘See you later,’ she whispered. ‘I’ll leave you here for when I get back, old friend.’ And she placed the doll back on the shelf.

Although Veena was grown up now, she looked so small with her big suitcases. Like her mother, Veena was fine-boned and short. Also like her mother, she was strong, energetic and a force to be reckoned with. Flying to Vancouver was Veena's first time on a plane. It took 24 hours to get there, changing flights in Tokyo.

When she arrived, it was August and summer in Canada, and yet the weather was so mild compared to Mumbai. That was the first shock. The next shock was the silence. Where was the traffic noise? Was everyone on holiday? The silence almost hurt her ears. She was so used to a city that was full to overloaded with vehicle noises and people everywhere that the quiet of Vancouver was a surprise.

She stayed temporarily with a family who helped her to feel at home and adjust to the big move. The backyard had beautiful soft lawn where Veena sat, enjoying that sense of freedom of finally being an adult out in the big world. As she read a textbook in the middle of the day, she thought, *I am making the decisions. I am independent and in control.*

When her studies commenced, Veena moved into a residential college on campus that couldn't have been more different from IIT. Her rooms were on the 14th floor with breathtaking views of the snow-capped Rocky mountains on one side and the Pacific Ocean on the other. This time she shared her residence with many other women studying across other subjects and faculties at the university. It was a lot of fun sharing with a such an interesting bunch of women. One night they dished up dessert and handed it to her. It was a whole tub of ice cream tipped onto a dinner plate!

'We know how much you like it,' they said, laughing. 'We thought this would be easier than going back for seconds and thirds and fourths … We thought – why not just eat the whole tub?'

Veena laughed and handed them all a spoon to share. It was so great to realise that student life didn't have to mean feeling isolated.

It was also while in Canada that Veena met Rama, who was studying for his **PhD** in Metallurgical Engineering. They had so much in common, and it was not long before they fell in love – although there was a potential clash because he was a clean freak and Veena continued to be quite messy. When Veena did the cleaning up, she always washed any containers that were usually put in the rubbish – like yoghurt or ice cream tubs or bottles that food came in – so they could be re-used. This was before recycling bins were introduced for everyday use.

'What are you doing? Just throw it in the bin,' Rama would say.

'No, I might use this to keep pens in. We shouldn't just throw everything in the rubbish.'

Their love was too strong to be ruined by such petty things, however, and soon they were writing home to their parents to tell them they were getting married.

'Say *cheese*!' The camera clicked.

Veena and Rama were trying to get good photos of each other to send to their parents. They both wanted to make a good impression.

Veena's parents were on the phone to her the minute they read her letter. They wanted to know more about this young man she planned to marry. Who were his family? What were his plans for the future? Veena assured them that Rama was lovely and kind. She also reminded them that she was an adult now.

Both the families agreed that the marriage was a wonderful idea and Veena and Rama flew back to India for the wedding, sharing their joy with their families. After Rama finished his PhD, he received the offer of a good job in Melbourne.

Veena had finished her master's and was studying for her PhD in Michigan in the USA which meant Rama and Veena would have to spend a year apart. Over her Christmas study break, Veena had time to fly to Melbourne to visit him. It was her first time in Australia, and she instantly felt as if she belonged. She loved the bright sunshine and heat that reminded her of Mumbai. There was a big Indian population that embraced her, too, and she found the people so friendly.

Fortunately, after finishing her PhD, Veena quickly found a job at the University of New South Wales, so she packed her microscope, goggles and

her lab coat and, with Rama, settled in Sydney. Of course, they would go home to Mumbai to visit their families each year, and soon they would take their twin daughters home to meet their grandparents! Having two babies was fun and tiring but it didn't slow Veena down at all.

13

Eureka!

It was around the year 2000 that Veena was wearing her hardhat, goggles, orange hi-vis vest and high-heeled ankle boots while traipsing around a rubbish tip. There was a warehouse, two-storeys high, with caged crates filled with squashed plastic bottles. Re-use, reduce and recycle was becoming an everyday slogan. But what about the plastics that couldn't be recycled?

Many people around the world were realising that plastics take thousands of years to break down and were causing immense damage to the air and soil because they were left in landfill or burnt. And they were also ending up in the rivers and the ocean.

Veena looked at the mountain of plastic bottles before her. *We're going to be inundated with this waste,* she thought. She had an almost overwhelming sense that she had to do something about it. *You have to ask the right questions*, she thought. *It isn't about asking, 'What is it?' I know what it is. It's a plastic bottle that is the wrong sort of plastic to recycle. I need to ask, 'What is the plastic bottle made out of and how can we get to those elements? What value could those elements have?'*

Steel is the world's most widely used construction material for making everyday items from cars to washing machines, cargo ships, buildings and surgical instruments.

Suddenly it felt as if there were a hundred thought bubbles above her head. The idea was very clear to her. How **steel** was made was over in one thought bubble, and over the other side, in another thought bubble, were the waste plastics. In her mind, Veena could connect the dots between them. Plastics have carbon in them. Carbon is an essential ingredient in steel, traditionally using carbon from coal after it has been turned into coke. Coal is a non-renewable **fossil fuel** and using fossil fuels contributes to climate change.

What if you used carbon from waste plastic to replace some of the carbon from fossil fuels in the process of making steel? This would be recycling *and* it would also reduce the use of fossil fuels. But would it work? In her mind she had already called it 'green steel'.

Veena had a new hypothesis.

'I think if we heat waste plastics or rubber at extremely high temperatures, it will make carbon material that can join with molten iron to make steel,' she told her team and other research scientists.

Even some of her team thought it was loopy and the industrial steelmakers certainly did. They said things like, 'What's wrong with using coal? It's cheap and available.'

Veena knew this was going to be a long-term solution but that it would require new ways of thinking. She knew it would take time. Firstly though, she had to prove it would work in the lab.

She was fortunate to receive a grant from the Australian Research Council (ARC) to investigate her theory. It was like getting the best toys she could imagine. In the lab she had all the equipment she needed and a wonderful team of research students. And now the experimenting could begin!

Veena had her hypothesis, but now she had to create an experiment that *showed* you could use plastic and iron ore to make steel, and then test it over and over until they could be certain that it worked. She set up monitors to capture the moment of transformation into steel so she could analyse it afterwards. But there were so many parts that they had to get right!

They had a small furnace about the size of an office printer which heated the iron and coke needed to make steel to temperatures over 1,550 degrees Celsius. They injected the ground-up waste plastic to replace some of the carbon (in the form of coke), experimenting with how much could be replaced, and waited for results. Because the furnace was so hot, her team had to watch what was happening through a monitor hooked up to the furnace to see right inside to the **smelting** process occurring. Sometimes all they could see was a screen of orange heat. An outsider watching them might have thought they were sitting around all day watching television. But they were literally witnessing the moment of transformation. It was in that small furnace that green steel was born.

At one stage, Veena was interviewed by a journalist for an article in the newspaper. After she showed him around the lab, he turned to her and said, 'Yeah, I can see you're passionate about it but, really, who would care? You can get dirt cheap coal in Australia.'

Negative opinions just emboldened her to prove that she could use recycled plastic waste to revolutionise the steel-making industry. She even thought that eventually she could perhaps replace *all* the coal in making steel. After all, she could see it in her head!

Her team ground up plastic and poured it into a glass beaker, combining it with varying amounts of coal, measuring it out carefully. Wearing white lab coats, goggles and gloves, Ishrad, one of the research students, would approach the furnace and open a small door. Using a long-armed tool to keep him away from the heat, he would put the substance into the furnace. And they would watch what happened.

Green steel, developed by Prof. Veena Sahajwalla, is created by replacing coal with end-of-life rubber tyres and waste plastic, and smelting at high temperatures with iron in an Electric Arc Furnace.

The research took the next six years. There were many, many failed experiments. The successes felt like magic. Veena and her team realised something exciting was happening when the mixture of coking coal and recycled plastics produced a more stable foamy **slag** compared to using only coal. This made the furnace burn more efficiently, while still making high quality steel. It was an unexpected bonus. The green steel not only used recycled materials – it was even more efficient to make than making steel from coal alone! It was an even bigger success than they imagined.

*

After all that hard work, in 2005 Veena and her team were so excited when they found out that they had been nominated for a prestigious **Eureka Award** for the invention of Green Steel.

'Oh, we're going to the Eureka Prize Award ceremony!' she said to Rama. 'I've been nominated. We'll have to dress up and look swish.'

Veena's team at the University were excited too. 'This is like the Oscars of Australian science!' said Saha, her colleague. 'Yes, it is!' said Veena, 'And we will be on the red carpet.'

That is exactly how it felt when they arrived at the Australian Museum in Sydney. Flashes going off as photos were taken. The whole event was even televised on the ABC. Everyone was dressed to the nines with glossy hair and shimmering jewellery. Rama wore a suit and Veena had a new red silk top. They walked into the big hall where tables were set out for dinner and drinks, each one with starched white cloth serviettes and a centrepiece of flowers. 'This is so fancy!' exclaimed Veena.

They found their table with their name cards on it. It was right at the back of the huge hall.

'Well, sitting back here I guess we're obviously not going to win anything!' she said to Rama. She pulled a face at her team because she knew they were all thinking the same thing. The stage was a long way to the front with two big screens behind the announcer showing close-ups of the announcements and recipients.

Veena was enjoying her dessert and asking Rama if she could have his, too, when the award was announced.

THE 2005 UNIVERSITY OF NSW EUREKA PRIZE FOR SCIENTIFIC RESEARCH GOES TO...

PROFESSOR VEENA SAHAJWALLA!

Rama had to nudge Veena off her chair. 'They've called your name!' he exclaimed.

Veena couldn't believe it. She smiled so much her face hurt. This was a huge achievement for her and her team. She walked to the stage in a daze as the crowd applauded and the camera zoomed closer.

She was in so much shock that she was waiting for the announcer to say it was a mistake. But it wasn't a mistake. She had won. And there she was, on stage, receiving her award, holding a large glass trophy. She would also receive prize money for her research.

Oh, my gosh! she thought. *Is this real?* she kept looking at her name engraved on the trophy as if to remind herself that she had really won.

*

After Veena got over the initial shock, and in the days following the award ceremony, she had mixed feelings. On the one hand she was, of course, very proud of her team of researchers. On the other hand, she felt a kind of embarrassment. There was still so much further to go! Still so much to prove! Making green steel successfully in a lab was one thing, but she wanted to see it work in the real world. That would involve partnering with industry and construction to make green steel a product that was used, trusted and produced in a way that created real change. She was still the ambitious Veena who wanted to change the world.

Not long afterwards, Veena was invited to an industry meeting of senior steelmakers at a steel plant. She agreed, thinking it would be interesting for her to get a look at the next step of manufacturing on a large scale. She thought she could sit there and be like a fly on the wall, listening and learning.

Dressed in her goggles, hard hat and hi-vis vest, she toured the plant and then opened the door to the meeting room. Men in suits were sitting around a long oval table, and as she entered, they all stood. She sat down and waited to hear what they had to say when, suddenly, it dawned on her that they were waiting for her! They were wanting to know about her research!

Although unprepared and with no presentation materials, she thought, *I have to take this chance. Here are all the people I need to convince that green steel could be made on an industrial scale.* So, without further hesitation, she launched in with her ideas.

'Making steel at over 1,600 degrees Celsius seems like the last place you would think of needing to use plastic waste. But plastic has something in it that is essential to making steel – carbon. But why? Why get rid of coke from coal? Australia has a huge coal industry and no lack of supply. Why would we do that? Coal is readily available and works. If it ain't broke, why fix it?'

The others chuckled. But Veena wasn't deterred.

'In our experiments we have proven that a third of the carbon can come from plastics and mixed with carbon from coal, makes a more stable steel product which has the added benefit of improving the energy efficiency of the furnace,' she told them.

'But where will we get the supply of plastic we need?' asked one of the men. 'Won't there be a cost in processing the plastic to get it ready for the furnace?'

It was true. The first hurdle was to source the recycled material to replace the carbon from coal. It takes roughly half a tonne of coal to make a tonne of steel. The ground-up plastics worked in the lab, but she would need something in much larger quantities that was easier to get and cost-effective.

'We can recycle old car tyres,' Veena told them. 'There are mountains of waste tyres. Even if you don't care about climate change and fossil fuels, we know that at least 20 million car tyres end up in landfill in Australia every year, so we have to do something about it.'

'Why do I care about recycling tyres? That's not my problem,' said another one of the steelmakers.

Oh, my gosh! Are you kidding me? thought Veena. She knew there were so many reasons to solve the problem of mountains of waste rubber tyres. They were causing a lot of harm each year, even catching on fire and causing terrible smoke pollution with dangerous particles in it. But she knew the way to convince the steel industry was that it made sense economically.

'The rubber is even better than coal. It contains other elements, like hydrogen, which assists iron oxide to convert into iron which means your furnace runs more efficiently,' she explained to them. 'Green steel using recycled rubber tyres will reduce the cost of your raw materials and make your furnace more productive. Bottom line, you will produce better steel at lower costs!'

That really made them all sit up.

Veena convinced a big steel company called One Steel, to start ground-breaking trials of making green steel on a large scale. What she had proven in the lab, she now had to prove in the real world.

And, amazingly, it worked! They were able to replace more than one third of the coal-based carbon with waste tyres.

But still Veena wanted to push the ideas further. She was sure she could do more!

That same year Veena established the **SMaRT Centre** at the University of New South Wales to focus on researching the recycling of materials and processes for manufacturing. This would be a place for pioneering the transformation of waste for a new generation of 'green' materials and products, not just steel.

Smart, huh!

SMaRT Centre stands for Centre for Sustainable Materials Research and Technology (SMaRT). It does research with industry and governments to develop innovative sustainable solutions for the world's biggest waste challenges.

14

Television star

'Standby, roll camera and action!' called the director.

'G'day, I'm James O'Loughlin and welcome to The New Inventors!'

James O'Loughlin, balding with glasses and wearing a dark suit and colourful shirt introduced the show. He was a well-known presenter and comedian with a ready laugh in his voice. The show? A very popular television show on ABC television where inventors showcased their ideas and products and were interrogated by three expert judges. The show ran for seven years from 2004 to 2011.

The set was bright pink and purple with organic-shaped screens in squares and a big, curved desk where three judges sat. James smiled at the camera as he introduced the expert panel of judges which tonight included engineer, Dr Veena Sahajwalla.

When the producers had approached Veena to be a judge on the show she jumped at the chance. She had seen The New Inventors, which aired weekly on Wednesday nights at 8 p.m. She loved the idea of people all around the country watching a show about science in their lounge rooms, especially a show that displayed just how creative, fun, and interesting science can be. It was only after she had said *yes* that she started to worry. While she was confident discussing science, ideas and innovative designs, she knew nothing about being a television presenter! And now here she was, about to record her first episode.

Earlier in the day she was a bundle of nerves. There was so much to learn. Where to look with the multiple cameras, speaking clearly and at the right volume. And then all the jargon of a television set. There were **gaffers** and **grips** and **boom operators**. And then there were the production designers and camera operators, **directors**, assistant directors and **producers**. Best of all there were also caterers!

Walking onto set to meet everyone was overwhelming. Could she really be on television and be articulate and not um and ah and stumble over her words while she knew a camera was focused on her face? Fortunately, there were rehearsals. And everyone was really, really helpful, especially James.

After rehearsal she quickly caught up with him.

'Excuse me, James, do you have any advice? Anything I could do better?' she asked.

James smiled at her saying, 'You'll be great! Just be yourself! That's all we want.'

Veena smiled and thanked him. She remembered what her mother always said to her – whatever you do, do your best. And she would do her best and try and improve every week she was on the show.

While in hair and makeup she looked over the script again, familiarising herself with the contestants' names and their inventions. She could barely contain her excitement!

'Oh, these inventions sound so good!' she said to the makeup artist. 'It's going to be such an intriguing episode!'

She was looking forward to meeting all the talented inventors and asking them questions about their ideas, processes, and their experiments. This was everything she loves about science! She hoped many of the young people watching would be inspired to study science too.

'Oh! Wow!' she said as she looked back at herself in the mirror. Her eyebrows went up and her eyes wide although she was smiling and knew she looked good. 'Don't you think the makeup is a bit much? I don't think my own family would recognise me!'

'Trust me,' said the makeup artist standing behind her, hands on Veena's shoulders. 'You need this much makeup under the lights. It will look really good on screen. Not too much at all.'

'On set in five minutes, Veena!' said the assistant director at the door.

Veena took a deep breath. She crossed her fingers. She hoped she wouldn't say the wrong thing or stumble over her words.

On set she met the contestants and shook their hands, noticing that they were far more nervous than she was. She quickly moved to make them feel at ease – helping them made her own nerves fade away.

'Places, please!' called the assistant director.

Veena smiled and wished the inventors good luck before taking her place behind the panel desk. Microphones were clipped onto lapels, battery packs attached at the back, the wire running down through their clothes. The makeup artists did final checks on everyone's faces and hair. The camera glided across the floor on their big stands, the operators riding on them.

'Here we go,' said James.

'I'm nervous!' said Veena

'You'll be terrific. I know it,' James answered.

All of sudden the cameras were rolling, the audience was applauding, James was talking and the show was happening. Veena found her nerves totally disappeared once she was talking science to the contestants. She was in her element. This was the world she knew – experimentation, creative thinking, trial and error. She had the ability to drill down and ask relevant questions, all while smiling and being excited for the inventor. She was genuinely interested, so it wasn't hard at all.

At the end of the episode, the theme music played, the audience clapped, the cameras zoomed away and the lights dimmed. They had made it.

The judges and contestants all laughed and chatted. Veena couldn't help asking even more questions. She was already looking forward to recording the next episode!

'Veena! You're a natural!' James exclaimed. 'Just wait till the television audience sees you. The camera loves you. Well done!'

'Thank you, James, you're too kind. There is still so much I need to learn. If you have any tips on how I can improve, please let me know.'

'I will, Veena, but for now, just keep doing what you're doing. Just wait until the show airs – you'll be receiving fan mail, I guarantee!' Veena laughed. James was such a nice, funny guy.

'Oh, I don't know about that! My kids are going to find Mummy on the TV very strange!'

James was right. When the show aired, many viewers expressed how much they enjoyed watching Veena. She really did light up the screen with her warmth, enthusiasm, intelligent questions – and, of course, her sparkling wide smile! He was right about the fan mail too. It was all very encouraging.

Veena was on the show for seven years, all the way until it was wrapped up. She admired the resourcefulness of the inventors, and her favourite inventions were the ones with practical applications that addressed big problems – safety, sustainability and farming. It was always inspiring to be around people with such creative innovations. She also knew the challenges they faced in getting their clever ideas into the marketplace and commercially viable because she was facing these challenges herself with green steel.

Over the years, James's antics as the host of The New Inventors would be legendary. Veena would never forget the time he crashed a small vehicle into the set, shouting, 'That didn't happen in rehearsal! Take two?' and the whole audience laughed uproariously. Then there was the time when a horse almost bit him, and the time he was dragged along by a dog sled, and the many times he went flying across the studio in various contraptions. Veena hadn't expected that the show would be so much fun and so popular. She never stopped trying to improve her own contribution as a judge, always asking James if she was doing okay.

The final episode was in 2011. Being an end-of-season show, it had all the weekly winners back on the set to award a winner for that last year. But it was also a great celebration of all they had achieved over the years with their Wednesday night television show that had inspired so many.

There was rousing applause from the audience and a tear in Veena's eye at the finale of this era of televised new inventions.

15

Recycling champion

Veena looked through the rubbish bin for any items that could be recycled.

'What are you doing, Veena?' asked Rama. 'I need to take the rubbish outside!'

'Not before I go through everything,' she said. 'What's this container doing in the bin? It should be recycled.'

'There you go, being the rubbish cop!' said Rama.

Veena laughed. 'Yes, that's what the twins always call me, too!'

Veena was always checking the recycling symbol on the bottom of the plastics, looking at what everything was made of. She started taking things out of the bin and putting them in her basket.

'You're hoarding rubbish, again,' said Rama.

'I'm not a hoarder. I'm curious. Look at this chip packet. The lining has aluminium in it. Maybe I could do something with that! I'm taking it into work.'

After the success of green steel, Veena was thinking about what other waste products needed to be revived, re-formed and reinvented into new materials. With so much waste in the world she couldn't stop. She was now a recycling champion.

At the SMaRT Centre she had a team of about 25 passionate young engineers and scientists working in waste recycling of all kinds. That morning, Veena wheeled her trolley of rubbish down the corridor.

'What have you got there, Veena?' asked Anirban, one of the research team. Keeping up with Veena was a challenge and Anirban was finding it hard.

'Lots of goodies!' she said with a grin. 'Let's show the others!'

Anirban loved working with Veena. He admired the way science, technology and engineering were part of everything she did, and the way her mind jumped from idea to idea.

'Look at this bag, Anirban,' she said, holding up a plastic net bag from oranges and giving the bag a tug. 'Look, it has really strong polymers.'

She was especially interested in things that weren't considered recyclable so were ending up in landfill.

'And look at this chip packet.' Veena passed the bag to him. Anirban peered inside.

'This is aluminium!' he exclaimed.

'Exactly! We need to look at that, don't you think?'

'Definitely. That's a good project,' Anirban answered.

'We just need to ask the right questions. What properties does it have? We just have to break things down to the elements and work out what we can mix together to create a new product. Waste is an opportunity! It is as an untouched resource waiting to be harnessed!'

Growing up in Mumbai, Veena knew that there was no such thing as waste. Everything had value and potential. She also knew that the planet was in a climate change crisis, and one of the major problems was waste. The 'reduce, re-use, recycle' slogan didn't go far enough.

Why can't we revive? she thought. Why can't we reinvent and re-form things?

An important trigger was an export ban on waste in 2018 which meant that Australia could no longer send rubbish overseas to be someone else's problem. *We have to solve it ourselves!* Veena thought. *We need to be bold and brave and think BIG!*

And she wasn't just thinking what could be recycled, but *how* it could be recycled in a way that was practical and would benefit local communities with jobs; that would change people's lives for the better. *What about micro-recycling and re-forming manufacturing plants?* Veena thought. This exciting new idea was another world first!

The concept of these mini factories was to revive and reinvent waste. It turned traditional manufacturing on its head. Veena's vision was that each mini factory could connect to other mini factories. This meant people could start small and then two or three businesses could work together on a shared solution with recycling. Manufacturing didn't have to be big business, it could be a collaboration of small businesses.

Her ultimate idea was that small communities – towns or suburbs or council areas – could deal with their own waste by recycling and re-forming through what she now called **MICROfactories**, providing jobs for the people who live there. It was so thrilling! Small scale but big impact! Once again, she had to prove her idea would work in the lab first.

A **MICROfactorie** is one or a series of small machines and devices that perform one or more functions to transform waste products into new and usable resources.

The team started to design components and machinery. In 2018, Veena and her team launched the world's first MICROfactorie at the SMaRT Centre. It was only 50 square metres or around four car spaces in size. She wanted to prove that in that small space she could build all the equipment needed to 'revive' waste into usable products.

'It's not just about the science, it's not just about technology,' she said to her team, 'it's about understanding that we can all play a part in healing our planet. As materials scientists and engineers, we need to think about what kind of materials go into making a product from the point of view of sustainability. It should never end up polluting our environment.'

The first waste challenge for the MICROfactories was **e-waste**, one of the fastest growing waste areas in the world. *We've got so many different types of electronics, computers and our phones. There are a lot of good quality plastics in there. And typically, a lot will end up going to landfill,* thought Veena. She knew this was the right challenge for her.

Veena and her team collected the discarded electronic devices, took them apart and placed the components into a machine to break them down into the various elements. What resulted were metals and plastics. The metals were put in a small furnace where they were transformed into valuable alloy materials that could later be used to make ceramics. The plastics were put through another module that produced filaments suitable for 3D-printing machines. It sounded simple but it took many experiments to get the temperature and quantities right for this to work.

The first thing the MICROfactorie produced was a pair of 3D-printed glasses frames. Veena designed them to be the iconic shape of **Mahatma Gandhi** glasses, small and round. Watching the 3D printer **extrude** the recycled plastic into small round glasses filled Veena with joy. It was an object that connected her innovation back to her roots in India. It also made a statement about how she wanted recycling manufacturing to be accessible to everybody, empowering people to recycle and create industry and jobs in their communities.

Mahatma Gandhi (1869-1948) was a lawyer, politician, social activist, and writer who became the leader of the nationalist independence movement against British rule in India. He is internationally admired for his philosophy of successful non-violent protest to achieve political and social progress.

But Veena wasn't finished. There was so much waste to be explored and used. Her next challenge was to create 'green' ceramics from waste products, combining glass and textiles in a MICROfactorie.

Australians discard close to 800,000 tonnes of clothing and textiles each year – 15 tonnes every 10 minutes!

Creating green ceramics involved a lot of experimentation which Veena, of course, found exciting. The product had to be long-lasting and have strength. She had to work out a way for the glass and textile to bond and stick together. They experimented with extreme temperatures and had many failures where she would pick up a tile that would fall apart in her hands. She had to think creatively and ask many questions.

'Is there something you could do when the tile comes out hot, to improve it and make it stronger?'

'How can we take advantage of everything that is inside a material, including taking advantage of the process of the heat?'

The team was always refining experiments.

Veena had clear, bold ideas but ideas alone are not enough. She had to make it practical too. She had to connect the dots for how to make green ceramics in a way that would work in the real world. Meanwhile, she and the team kept experimenting.

Finally, one day it worked. She had invented a new product that combined the textiles from old clothes with glass and turned them into products for the building industry. She called it Green Ceramics. The next challenge was to produce it and make it available for people to buy and use in their homes.

In 2019 she partnered with a property developer and designers to use her products in real apartments. When Veena walked into the display apartment that incorporated her products, she was covered in goosebumps.

'Oh, my gosh!' she gasped.

Here was a room made from recycled products invented and produced in her MICROfactorie. They had created flooring, wall coverings, bowls, tables, benchtops and even artwork for the walls. It was wonderful! It was a culmination of the resourcefulness she saw in the people of Mumbai, transformed with her scientific expertise and combined with good designs, into something valuable, practical and beautiful too.

Oh wow! she kept saying to herself.

*

'If you can do it here in Cootamundra, you can do it anywhere!' Veena said to her friend, Andrew.

Andrew was setting up the very first MICROfactorie in real life in the small town of Cootamundra in country New South Wales. The SMaRT Centre had a grant to help, and Veena and her team had been working hard to set it up. The property developers Veena had partnered with were building an apartment complex on the site of the old Channel 9 television studios in Sydney. Andrew had been collecting all the waste products from the old site to use in this first MICROfactorie to manufacture Green Ceramics that would be used in the new apartments.

In March 2021, Veena's vision of a MICROfactorie became a reality. It was time to hit the button and set the machinery working. It was so exciting for Veena, her team and Andrew, to have this moment finally happen.

'You press the button,' Andrew said to Veena.

'No, *you* should, Andrew,' said Veena. 'This is *your* MICROfactorie!'

'Let's do it together,' said Andrew. And they did. Pressing 'Go' on the world's first operating recycling MICROfactorie.

The very first square tile to come out of the machine was brilliant. The team couldn't stop laughing together. It was a magical day.

'Now we can roll out MICROfactories across Australia!' Veena said to her team.

Veena's creative thinking with waste recycling was now so much more. It was a mini-industrial revolution! Veena had invented products and a way of making them so that it was possible for small communities to set up their own recycling manufacturing businesses.

Veena had a vision that every community could have a MICROfactorie so that nothing went waste, and everything was a resource to be used! A future where there was no such thing as waste! Veena's vision was a zero-waste economy that not only dealt with textile waste, glass waste and e-waste but *all* our problematic waste.

She felt Australia was on the cusp of that change and she had proven, through science, how it could happen. No longer would the world be confined to, 're-use, reduce, recycle'. She had shown how to 'revive, reinvent, re-form and revolutionise!'

*

Over the years, Veena wasn't only thinking about innovation in recycling. In 2015 she was one of the founders of the **Science 50:50 program**, which was part of the **Girls in Science** initiative at the University of New South Wales. Remembering the challenges she faced as a woman studying and working in engineering, Veena could see how to help girls pursue careers in science. From internships to industry scholarships and mentoring, she wanted to help foster an inclusive culture where women could thrive as scientists.

The Science 50:50 program encourages girls to pursue careers in science through university visits, opportunities to write blogs and attend excursions to industrial sites. Veena thought of her friend, Panna, and how, if she had had this sort of encouragement when she was at school, then maybe she, too, would have sat that exam and become an engineer.

In the early days of Green Steel, Veena was truly ahead of the times. But 20 years later, amid a growing awareness around the world of the human-made climate crisis, especially with the catastrophic floods, fires and extreme weather events, her vision of producing sustainable products that reduce fossil fuels' use and waste, is now even more important and urgent.

Her dream of making Green Steel on an industrial level came true, both in Australia and overseas. But in true Veena style, she continued to improve the process. With further research and experimentation, she was able to not only cut down the amount of carbon in steel from coal, but she was able to replace coal altogether! It was a world first. By 2021 green steel had saved millions of tyres going into landfill. But that didn't mean the end of ideas. She even wondered, *Could coffee waste be used for making steel?*

Veena has been able to pursue her ideas and experiments with the support of the Australian Research Council, The University of New South Wales and through the National Environmental Science Program (NESP), where Veena became the Leader of the Sustainable Communities and Waste Hub. This is a group of world-class research institutions, industry, government and community organisations which seek solutions for waste reduction and a more sustainable world. Veena never stopped thinking about creative ways to meet environmental challenges and working hard to invent, innovate and inspire others.

In 2022, she was named NSW Australian of the Year. Then, in the same year, she was awarded another Eureka Prize, this time for Promoting Understanding of Science!

Growing up in Mumbai, Veena Sahajwalla learnt there was value in rubbish. Becoming an engineer gave her the skills to innovate and find solutions that were both bold in the laboratory and practical in the real world. Her curiosity and determination to change lives and help the planet made her think creatively and find ambitious solutions. She always had the courage to try, experiment, fail and try again – and to ask the difficult questions. And now Professor Veena Sahajwalla has become a global scientific innovator, an inventor, a materials revolutionary and a recycling champion!

Glossary

- **Boom operators** – hold and move the boom microphones on long poles, for film or television recording.
- **Chai tea** – 'chai' is the Hindi word for tea. In India it is a hot drink made from tea and spices, mixed with milk and sugar.
- **Coke** – is a solid hard product made by heating coal at very high temperatures to concentrate the carbon.
- **Director** – directs performers, cameras and crew on a film or television set.
- **Eureka moment** – a moment when you have a sudden realisation/bright idea or when a solution to a problem comes to mind. 'Eureka' comes from a Greek word, heureka, meaning, 'I found it!'
- **Eureka Prize** – is awarded each year by the Australian Museum to individuals and organisations for excellence in innovation and research in science in Australia.
- **E-waste** – or electronic waste is discarded electronic appliances such as mobile phones, computers, and televisions. E-waste is any item with a plug, battery or power cord that's no longer working or wanted. The world produces 50 million tonnes of e-waste a year.

- **Extrude** – means to force, press or push out.
- **Fossil fuels** – are biological materials that exist within Earth's crust and contain hydrocarbons that can be used as a source of energy. Fossil fuels include coal, petroleum, natural gas, oil shales, bitumen, tar sands, and heavy oils.
- **Gaffers** – lighting technicians on a film or television set.
- **Ghee** – is butter that has been melted to separate the liquid fats from milk solids which are removed. It is also called clarified butter.
- **Grips** – people on a film or television set who are responsible for setting up and operating moving camera equipment, such as a crane.
- **Gulab jarmun** – is a dessert made from round sponge-like dumplings, golden fried and then soaked in sugar syrup.
- **Lecturer** – a person who gives lectures, a teacher at university.
- **Lecture theatre** – place where students attend lectures at university – usually tiered like a performance theatre.
- **PhD** – means Doctor of Philosophy. It is a high level of postgraduate research in a particular area that is undertaken after completing undergraduate studies. It usually takes about 4 years to complete.

- **Pride and Prejudice** is a famous novel written by Jane Austen in 1813. It is the story of Elizabeth Bennet and her four sisters and parents, and her journey to get married. Their mother, Mrs Bennet, has dramatic and manipulative mood swings and a great determination to see all her daughters married. The family's world is turned upside down by the arrival of eligible bachelors, Mr Darcy and Mr Bingley, and their fortunes are entwined.
- **Process metallurgist** – scientist who oversees, develops and tests processes used in making metals.
- **Producer** – person who oversees and organises the logistics for a film or television production.
- **Sherlock Holmes and Dr Watson** – fictional characters created by the famous English writer Arthur Conan Doyle, who wrote 62 Sherlock Holmes stories during the years 1887-1927. Sherlock Holmes is an eccentric private detective and Dr Watson is his not-as-smart, but loyal assistant. Many of the stories have been released as TV series and feature films.
- **Smelting** – is the process of applying heat to create steel.
- **Tandoori** – is a method of cooking meat and vegetables in a wood-fired clay oven that comes from the Punjabi area of India. It is now popular all over the world.

About Julianne Negri

Julianne Negri's debut children's novel *The Secret Library of Hummingbird House* was published in 2020 and was a 2021 CBCA Notable. Julianne works in children and youth programming for Public Libraries and has been a musician, eco-crafter, filmmaker, television host and is the mother of five children. Julianne likes to have hair the colour of the sunset – all tones of pink, orange and mauve, and her favourite thing in the world is her dog, Rocket.